ALMOST AUTUMN

MARIANNE KAURIN

TRANSLATED FROM THE NORWEGIAN BY

ROSIE HEDGER

Arthur A. Levine Books

An Imprint of Scholastic Inc.

Originally published in Norwegian in 2012 as *Nærmere høst*
by H. Aschehoug & Co.

Library of Congress Cataloging-in-Publication Data

Names: Kaurin, Marianne, 1974– author. | Hedger, Rosie, translator.
Title: Almost autumn / Marianne Kaurin ; translated from the Norwegian by
  Rosie Hedger.
Other titles: Nærmere høst. English
Description: First American edition. | New York, NY : Arthur A. Levine Books,
  an imprint of Scholastic Inc., 2017. | "Originally published in Norwegian in
  2012 as Nærmere høst by H. Aschehoug & Co."—Copyright page. | Summary:
  As autumn approaches Ilse Stern is thinking about her infatuation with
  Hermann Rød, and whether his determination to be a painter will interfere
  with their romance—but the reality of being Jewish in occupied Oslo is about
  to turn her whole world upside down, as the deportation of the Norwegian
  Jews begins. | Includes bibliographical references.
Identifiers: LCCN 2016025310 | ISBN 9780545889650 (jacketed hardcover :
  alk. paper)
Subjects: LCSH: Jewish teenagers—Norway—Oslo—Juvenile fiction. |
  Antisemitism—Norway—Juvenile fiction. | Holocaust, Jewish (1939–1945)—
  Norway—Oslo—Juvenile fiction. | Norway—History—German occupation,
  1940–1945—Juvenile fiction. | Oslo (Norway)—History—20th century—
  Juvenile fiction. | CYAC: Jews—Norway—Oslo—Fiction. | Antisemitism—
  Fiction. | Holocaust, Jewish (1939–1945)—Norway—Oslo—Fiction. | Norway—
  History—German occupation, 1940–1945—Fiction. | Oslo (Norway)—
  History—20th century—Fiction.
Classification: LCC PZ7.1.K38 Al 2017 | DDC 839.823/8 [Fic]—dc23
LC record available at https://lccn.loc.gov/2016025310

10 9 8 7 6 5 4 3 2 1   17 18 19 20 21
Printed in the U.S.A. 23

First American edition, January 2017

Book design by Elizabeth B. Parisi

To Jens, Maren, and Liv

S UMMER IS OVER.

The leaves in the dusty streets congregate in great piles along the tenement buildings, dry and crisp, yellow and red, all awaiting inevitable disintegration. The air is bracing and tinged with something, a scent, a rupture. Before long the wind will gather pace and the rain will pour, hammering against windows and asphalt, creating deep furrows in the gravel. Before long the earth will become damp and cold, teeming with reptiles, worms, and beetles that eagerly take all that they need from the soil. Before long the ground will become hard and impenetrable; before long there will be snow. A hard shell will form over the freezing water and white, frosty, rigid blades of grass, giving rest to all that is dead.

The sun continues to shine, faint and low in the sky, the light falling at an angle across a gateway in the Grünerløkka district of Oslo. Out of the gate emerges Ilse Stern. She walks quickly, smiling. She turns around where she stands on Biermanns gate, the street she's lived on her whole life. The gray tenement building stands like an empty shell in the dwindling afternoon light, a dormant wall of bricks and closed windows. From the outside it looks like any other tenement building. Four floors, dark curtains, a wrought-iron gate leading to a passageway that houses rubbish bins and a shady backyard beyond it. There is no movement to be seen in the windows of the third floor. From outside it is impossible to see all that moves inside, every breath and pulse and life within.

Ilse hurries around the corner and out onto Toftes gate. She has done it. She has successfully made her way out of the apartment without her mother ruining her plans with her usual incessant nagging. Not a word about her inconsiderate attitude, or how she only thinks of herself, no demands to consider this or that or the other, and nothing about being back at home before curfew.

They were both having a snooze after their meal when she left, her mother and father snoring in perfect harmony. Sonja and Miriam were in Torshovdalen Park. Miriam had pestered Ilse to go with them, please Ilse, come with us, we can race each other down the hill. Ha! As if a race at Torshovdalen Park could measure up to Ilse's plans for that Saturday afternoon; what kind of suggestion was that, today of all days?

Like a snake, Ilse had slithered stealthily around the cramped apartment to avoid waking her snoozing parents, their heads lolling forward as they napped. Her mother's handbag hung on one of the pegs in the hallway. Ilse looped the handle over the hook and carefully opened it, rummaging around in the tangle of tissues and receipts until she finally located what she was looking for. She stood before the kitchen mirror and applied the lipstick in thick layers. She pouted, cocked her head to one side, closed her eyes, felt the cool of the glass mirror reflect back onto her face, watched as her breath created a light film of condensation on the surface. Red, pink, full-lipped, ready for kissing. She had brushed her hair one hundred times, first on one side and then the other. She had gazed at her reflection for a long while, checking her profile from the right-hand side and smiling. The kitchen floor was covered in dark hair by the time she had finished. Her mother didn't like it when she brushed her hair in the kitchen; it's unhygienic, Ilse, you'll get hair in our food. Ilse bent over to pick up the stray hairs, gathering them into a ball in her hand and throwing them in the bin. She left a note on the kitchen table before leaving: "Out for a walk." No further explanation.

She feels the warmth of the sun on her face and basks in the light, dust blowing up from the road and the leaves crackling beneath her feet as she wades through them. Toftes gate stretches out before her like a broad avenue; she just needs to follow the road down and straight ahead. She is on her way. Everything begins now. She is wearing her summer dress, the white one with red polka dots that Sonja sewed for her; it's too late in the year to be wearing such a lightweight dress, she knows that, but all the same, if there is one day to wear her summer dress, to really show off her best side, that day is today. It has short sleeves and is made from fine cotton, and one day during the summer, well, on the sixteenth of July at just past four o'clock in the afternoon, to be exact, Hermann had seen her wearing it and had commented on how well it suited her. Now she feels the way that the cold air blows through the fabric, goose bumps rising, the fine hairs on her bare forearms standing up like black antennae. She'll have to keep her arms behind her back so he won't notice.

Ilse quickens her pace as she makes her way along the narrow footpaths through Birkelunden Park. There is no music playing in the pavilion today, there hasn't been for some time now. Her family often used to spend their Sundays here with many of their neighbors from the same building on Biermanns gate; food in baskets, bottles of pop, and plenty of blankets to go around. She and Sonja would run around with Hermann and Dagny and the other children. Ole Rustad from the fourth floor would ask his wife to dance, moving across the grass with aplomb as he sang and everyone laughed. Things are so different now, so quiet; everyone seems to be on their guard. Paulus Church is just across the street. She looks up at the spire. When she was young, Sonja had convinced her that a man lived up there, a servant in the church with a wooden leg and long, tangled hair. Sonja had told her that the man held a girl captive in a specially created dungeon, starving her until she was no more than a skeleton in spectacles—because she had spectacles, the girl in the story. Ilse had always squeezed Sonja's hand tightly as they crossed through Birkelunden Park, right up until she must have been twelve years old. She had had so many nightmares about the bespectacled skeleton, had taken so many detours to avoid this very place.

The large birch trees whisper in the wind. The streets seem wider than usual; there is less dust, less litter. There are four words in her head, four words that have popped up out of nowhere, like a chorus, a march: Everything starts this autumn. Everything starts this autumn. One, two, three, four. Everything starts this autumn. Something is waiting for her; *someone* is waiting for her. The leaves may plummet from the treetops, the earth may become hard and impenetrable, the rain may fall and the wind may tear through the streets, and the war, the stupid war, it can carry on regardless, because she, Ilse Stern, fifteen and a half years old and in her summer dress and lipstick, she is heading for something warm and red that beats strong, and there is nothing that can stop her.

People sit chatting in Olaf Ryes Square, some on the grass and others on the green benches positioned in a semicircle around the fountain. Water continues to gurgle and the tall trees cast shadows over the open square where children play tag, running after one another as they laugh and squeal. It seems so long ago that she was one of them, a scruffy little city child with skinny pigtails, darting around in the streets and parks of Grünerløkka.

Ilse looks for a slender boy with fair, bristly hair and a gap between his front teeth, a boy with delicate, dry hands and a familiar stroll, a boy who smells like Hermann. He is nowhere to be seen. The wind rustles in the trees. She waits.

A few days prior to this, at quarter past six on Tuesday evening, to be exact, she had heard a knock on her front door. He stood casually in the stairwell, one hand concealed behind his back.

"Ilse Stern," he said, as he always did. Except this wasn't quite like every other time; there was something different about his voice this time, something new.

"Hermann Rød," she replied.

Both fell silent for a moment. Ilse Stern and Hermann Rød. Neither said a word. Ilse stepped out into the stairwell, closing the door behind her. Her mother was sulking in the living room following an argument with

Ilse, no doubt gearing up for her next attack. Was that why Hermann had come; had she and her mother really argued *that* loudly? Her mother's voice had reached falsetto levels when she had found out about the flour; what kind of nonsense of yours is this, Ilse, smearing flour all over your face? It was a stupid argument, one of many. Had Hermann been at home, listening to them both as they had screamed at each other? Did she still have any flour on her face? She quickly wiped her cheek.

"What is it, Hermann?" she asked, a hint of uncertainty in her voice.

He drew his hand out from behind his back to reveal two slips of paper, waving them in the air before leaning in close to her.

"Meet me at the pictures on Saturday, five o'clock," Hermann said. "Row seven, seats eight and nine."

Since then she had imagined it all so clearly: Hermann appearing under the canopy of trees as she sits on the bench looking summery in her favorite polka dot dress, the way he gently places his arm around her shoulders and leads her into the darkness of the pictures.

Oh no, the family from the fourth floor are out for a walk, all of them, the girls running in front and Mr. and Mrs. Rustad not far behind them. Why didn't she bring a handbag? She could have rummaged through the contents or casually read a book. If only she could hide somehow; she doesn't want to talk to them, not now. Ole Rustad always makes such a fuss about nothing, joking and laughing, well well well, sitting here in your summer dress, Ilse Stern, we'll have to tell your mother about this, and who exactly are you waiting for? Ilse turns away, pretends to have discovered something interesting hovering between the tree trunks, moves as if to look more closely, but it's too late, it's no good, they've already seen her. Ole lifts his hand and begins waving frantically; Karin and Lilly come running toward her.

"Goodness me," says Ole Rustad, an inquisitive look on his face. "Is that the young Miss Stern in lonely full bloom?"

Why does he have to talk like that, making everything sound so over the top?

"And who is to have the pleasure of your company this evening, my dear?"

Of course. He just had to ask. She doesn't want to tell him that it's the boy next door that she's waiting for, all dressed up and blue with the cold.

"Greta Green," she quickly replies without thinking.

"Oh really? Greta Green, eh?" Ole repeats, winking mischievously back at her.

Greta Green. Where on earth did she pull that name from?

Another half hour passes. She sees no sign of his saunter, his thick, fair hair blowing in the breeze, she can't smell his Hermann-like scent, and a queue has begun to form outside the cinema. Was it in the park that they had agreed to meet? Or outside the cinema, perhaps? Suddenly she feels unsure, was it five o'clock, row seven, seats eight and nine? On the board outside she can see that the film is due to be screened twice that evening — once at five o'clock and again at seven o'clock. The doors open and the audience files in. Ilse remains alone outside. Her legs are trembling slightly, the hairs on her arms standing up like tiny black barbs; could it possibly have been seven o'clock, row five, seats eight and nine?

SUMMER. IT HAS BEEN SO BEAUTIFUL. Long, warm days, the sun baking hot and high in the sky above the tenement buildings. Afternoons spent in the cool shade of the lilac tree in the backyard, insects buzzing, Ilse seated on the bench beneath the tree with an open book in her lap. She could just as well have been reading a Chinese dictionary or her mother's knitting patterns for what it was worth, as the words transformed into tiny black reptiles, inching off the pages, creeping hastily or in their own good time as Ilse stared at the windows to the right-hand side of the third floor of their building. If he were in there then he'd soon catch sight of her, lean out of his kitchen window, call out to her, wave, come down? The creaking of the window latch, footsteps over the wooden floorboards of the passageway, voices, the thud of the building door, the clang of the wrought-iron gate—she analyzed every signal, sat upright, held the book open before her. Her eyes peered out over the top like those of a soldier in a trench, keenly observing everyone who walked from the gate to the door and the door to the gate. And when Hermann appeared, whether coming home or leaving, then she would be there; quite by chance and perfectly poised, an ornamental plant that had suddenly blossomed in the gray backyard. She rested the book in her lap for a moment, shifting ever so slightly to the left to make space for him beside her on her right; her right side was her best side, her profile looked more mature from that angle, he had to see her at her best. They could sit that way for hours. The sun disappeared over the rooftops of the tenement buildings leading toward Vogts gate, the air was cool, there was dew on the grass, they laughed, talked, close to each other on the bench where they sat. Her mother had a habit of interrupting things by leaning out of the bedroom window and waving Ilse inside with quick, irritating hand gestures.

"Do you know what?" he said one day as they sat in the same spot. He looked at her, smiled cautiously, secretive, as if there was something he simply couldn't resist telling her. Could this be the moment he would — what was it they always said in her books? — *despair* his love for her? At the end of every novel that she read there was always a scene like that; the young couple were brought together and all the loose ends in the story were neatly tied up. She straightened up, readied herself, shook her head.

"I'm starting an apprenticeship with a painter."

A tiny stab of disappointment.

"A painter?"

He nodded.

She couldn't picture it. Hermann had never told her that he could paint or draw; he'd never had any interests of that kind. A painter? Maybe there were things she didn't know about him, no matter how close they were.

"Why?"

"Because I want to," he said. "And now the opportunity has come up. I'm starting next week."

Ilse didn't know what to say. Congratulations, how nice for you, at least now you won't be destined to heave crates of beer around forever? She knew how much he hated his work at the brewery. She looked at him. Hermann Rød, the world-famous painter from Grünerløkka, son of a working-class family who now spent his days frequenting splendid cafés; popular, highly acclaimed, yet eternally faithful to the woman who never failed to stand by him through thick and thin: the beautiful Ilse Stern.

"What are you thinking about, Ilse?"

She looked at him. His clear blue eyes told of his combined excitement and trepidation.

"What does your dad have to say about it?" she asked him after a moment.

Hermann furrowed his brow, his white-blond eyebrows curling upward.

"I haven't told him yet," he replied, picking at the dried paint on the bench. "But I don't imagine he'll like it much."

Ilse had no trouble imagining that to be true: Hermann's father, a burly man who had dedicated his life to his work at the Ringnes brewery, securing his own son a job there, a proper job as far as he saw it, and that same son now fancied taking up painting. No, Tinius probably wouldn't be overjoyed at the prospect.

But that was what she liked so much about Hermann. He made his own decisions; he did what *he* wanted to do. Perhaps he had discovered that he was an artist at heart, and that his work at the brewery wasn't right for him; maybe this had been a long-held dream of his without him ever uttering a word about it to anyone. And so he went for it all the same, because he wanted to.

"Good luck," she said, as she caught sight of her mother's hands waving from the open bedroom window.

It was something that had sneaked up on her that summer, something that she hadn't been prepared for, but now there it was, it had latched on, like an insect savoring sweet, fresh blood. Love. Everything that she had read about it, everything that she had readied herself for, all she had imagined, and yet here it was. Would it really appear here, in a backyard in Grünerløkka, in a dark passageway that smelled of all the things that people threw out, in the same place where they used to catch rats and mice? They had lived side by side all their lives, each in their own family's apartment on the third floor of number ten Biermanns gate, three steps separating the door of one apartment from the door of the other. They had been married beneath the lavender tree when she was five and he was seven. Dagny Larsen from the first floor had presided over the ceremony; do you take this woman to be your lawfully wedded wife, she had solemnly asked, giggling with the other children who stood in a circle around the couple. I do, Hermann had announced loud and clear, and then Dagny had told them that they had to kiss, everybody had to when they got married, how horrible, Ilse had been having such fun up until the part with the kissing, she had cast aside her dandelion bouquet and hidden in the building's basement.

Hermann Rød. The hero. A hero who wasn't tall and olive-skinned, like they usually were in novels. Ilse said no when she meant yes and yes when she meant no, her palms were prone to sweating, and it was an effort simply to coordinate the movement of her arms and legs. And suddenly there she sat, glued fast to the gray planks every afternoon on the bench under the lavender tree, waiting. They were friends. Oh yes. But at the same time, wasn't there something about his hands, his rough fingers, the way they stroked her arm, the way that he always nudged her as they chatted; was it purely coincidental?

And now here she is, wet through in the passageway and with no idea what to think. She had waited for the next show to start, queued up yet again, hoped that she had made an error, that perhaps it *was* seven o'clock, row five, seats eight and nine that he had said after all. Two men in uniform had approached her, spoken to her in German, offered her a cigarette. She had turned away, the two men had continued walking, but then they had stopped a little way from her, stood there and stared at her, and they had laughed, yes, they had so obviously laughed at her. In the light from the windows of the cinema she had seen her own reflection: pale with pursed lips, her wet hair sticking to her face, her body shapeless and scrawny, trembling with cold in her polka dot dress. She had felt the rain tickling her hairline, the damp, heavy air and the steam rising from the pavement.

Her skirt and jacket lie behind the waste bin in a crumpled pile. The plan had been so clear when she had left the house that afternoon, her mother would never know a thing about the summer dress, she would change into her jacket and skirt before entering the apartment upon her return, but it hadn't occurred to her that it might rain. Should she put her jacket and skirt on over the wet dress, or change out of the dress first? She pulls the dry clothing on top of the dress, which clings to her body. It is late, far too late; why had she waited like that at Olaf Ryes Square?

She is sure she can hear her mother's voice even from where she stands in the stairwell, short-tempered, thorny, accusatory; she already knows what to expect. She is thoughtless, she has no consideration for others, she can't saunter around in the belief that she can come and go as she pleases, she is a member of this family and she has to follow the same rules as everyone else. Then the accusations, the pokes and prods at her guilty conscience. They've been so worried, her mother was close to a nervous breakdown, any one of these days the stress might break her, she could just snap in two, behaving this way just isn't acceptable.

As she reaches the third floor she leans in close to the door of the neighboring apartment. Silence within. Complete and utter silence. She just doesn't get it; why didn't he come? He had stood there in front of her, tickets in hand, bought and paid for, five o'clock, row seven, seats eight and nine, she just knows it, she can recite the words by heart. Her summer dress and lipstick, the way she had run along the streets, everything starts this autumn, ugh, she feels embarrassed at the mere thought. She certainly won't tell Hermann that she waited so long for him, he can never know. If he had forgotten about her then she can forget about him too, exclude him from her thoughts, banished, gone.

She takes a deep breath before reaching for the door handle. Hello, she calls out as cheerfully as she is able, stepping into the narrow hallway.

ERMANN LINGERS FOR SOME TIME outside Ilse's door when he arrives home that evening. In one hand he holds the painting; the other is free. He clenches his fist, his knuckles red and dry. Should he knock? Does he dare? He had imagined that he'd feel calm, as long as he made it home, as long as he made it in through the gate, up the stairs, snatched a moment to compose himself, to shake off his fear. He really thought he might feel clear, determined, firm.

There is silence within the apartment. Not a sound to be heard. Is she still awake? No, it's late, she must have gone to bed by now. If he were to knock then he'd have to explain why he hadn't turned up, and he can't do that. That is to say, he knows why he couldn't come, but an explanation that Ilse would believe, something reasonable and straightforward? That's not something he's managed to come up with quite yet.

He makes his way to his own front door and lets himself in.

The room is dimly lit. The blackout curtains have been drawn, but a lamp continues to burn. His father sits in the armchair by the window. The lamplight illuminates his face, which takes on an unexpectedly soft hue in the dim room. His father is in his string undershirt, his large belly expanding like a taut ball as he breathes in, his chest hairs sticking out through the holes in his shirt. On the table before him are two empty beer bottles and one half full. He takes it easy on Saturday evenings, never drinking until he's drunk but instead sitting in his armchair and enjoying large, greedy gulps of his beer. He always used to listen to the radio; he would sit and hum to himself, snapping his fingers to the beat. Now he simply sits, drinking his beer and staring blankly ahead.

"Father?"

Hermann places his hand gently on his father's shoulder.

"Father? Shouldn't you head to bed?"

His father jumps, sitting up abruptly in his chair and looking at Hermann as if he were a stranger.

"There you are," he says after a moment. "What time do you call this?"

He wipes his mouth, drawing one hand over his face for a moment before reaching out for the half-full bottle and taking a swig.

"I know it's late. I hope you weren't waiting up for me."

"Not me, son," he responds. "I'd spend a lot of my life in this chair if I made a habit of waiting for you to come home."

"Have you had a good evening?" Hermann asks, somewhat hesitantly.

"No," his father replies shortly.

"Sorry to hear that—why not?"

His father gives a resigned groan, drawing shallow breaths and shaking his head.

"Your mother's been out of her mind with worry all evening. We're getting tired of you not telling us where you disappear off to. Then Mr. Stern came over here asking if you were with Ilse."

Hermann can tell from his father's intonation that the final utterance is more a question than a statement. Hermann had intended to tell his father that he'd been out with Ilse, at the pictures and then for a walk, that time had just run away from them. That won't work now. He'll be caught out.

"I've been in Frogner," he says. Plan B. "Didn't I tell you?"

He holds up the painting as evidence, a watercolor landscape in various shades of pastel.

"Did you paint that?"

"I did," Hermann replies, "what do you think?"

His father snorts.

"I've always said that I don't know a thing about art. Anyway, what sort of class goes on at this time on a Saturday night?"

Hermann says nothing. He doesn't know what to say. No matter his explanation, it will be wrong and his father will resort to the same old comebacks. What was the point in these artistic endeavors, where did Hermann's sudden interest come from, wasn't his work at the brewery enough to keep him busy, was he suddenly too good for all that?

All through the summer Hermann had wondered how he should explain things to his father. First he'd told Ilse. She seemed to find the whole idea exciting. A little strange, perhaps, that he'd kept his talent a secret for all this time, but overall she had seemed impressed. His father, however, reacted somewhat differently.

"A painter?" he blurted. "Did I hear you right? You want to start an apprenticeship with a *painter*?"

He almost spat out the words, as if they were a poison that he couldn't rid himself of quickly enough.

"Yes," Hermann replied. "I've always wanted to learn to paint."

His father stared at him, openmouthed. He called

Hermann's mother into the room and pointed at Hermann as if he were a rare species of animal in a cage on display.

"The lad's going to take up painting," he boomed, pointing a quivering finger at Hermann's face. "Do you hear that, Ingeborg? He's taking up painting!"

His mother stared, equally openmouthed upon hearing the news. The way they were reacting it was clear that Hermann could just as well have admitted to having shot a man or announced his imminent departure for an expedition to the North Pole.

"And how do you plan on going about this?" his father asked.

"What do you mean?"

"What I *mean*," he repeated in a mocking tone, "is that you have work to attend to. When exactly are you planning on carrying on with this painting malarkey?"

"In the afternoons," Hermann replied. "It's on the other side of town, in Frogner."

"Oh, *I see*, in *Frogner* is it," his father replied sarcastically. "I suppose they have plenty of time for that sort of thing on the posh side of town."

"I won't let it affect my work," Hermann mumbled.

But it had affected his work. On several occasions he had arrived late, lacked concentration, and fought sleep deprivation after a long night spent on the other side of the city. Once he had lost his grip while transporting a load and twenty-four bottles of beer had come crashing to the floor, smashing into pieces all around him. He felt the foreman's eyes boring holes into him, clearly suspicious—a suspicion he couldn't escape, even at home. His mother would swoop in toward him, smelling his breath. She and his father had convinced themselves that he was drinking too much, spending his time taking booze-fueled wanders on the west side of the city, and that this must be the reason for his late returns each night.

His father shuffles across the room and into his bedroom, closing the door behind him without saying good night. Hermann tidies up in the living room, unfolds the bedsheet, and lays it out over the sofa before fetching his bedcovers from the blue chest. He lies there for a long while, his eyes fixed on a crack in the painted ceiling.

If Isak had come looking for Ilse it meant only one thing: She hadn't come home either. Maybe she'd stood there and waited for him; he can see her now, wonders what she's thinking. If he knows her as well as he thinks, there will be no shortage of thoughts racing through her head. She can be so dramatic, she'll no doubt have concocted all manner of stories to explain his absence. Perhaps she'd been afraid for him, imagined that something might have happened to him. He feels warm for a moment as the thought occurs to him.

He wonders what he'll tell her when they next meet. How will he work his way out of this? Won't Ilse be suspicious? There are so many things to keep on top of, so many versions of everything all the time. It's as if he's dragging a bureau with an endless number of drawers around behind him, and he has to be constantly aware of exactly which drawer he is opening and which he has to keep closed. He won't have a chance to speak to her tomorrow morning either: At ten o'clock he has to be back in Frogner with Einar Vindju. We have a lot to do now, Einar had told Hermann before he left this evening.

Hermann had walked all the way to Frogner that day. The air was cold and crisp but the sun shone, suspended over the city, faint and far off, gently warming the earth below. He arrived at the building on the corner of Frederik Stangs gate, giving three short, sharp rings on the bell. Einar Vindju stood in his doorway when Hermann reached the top of the stairs. Inside the apartment, the glass doors leading into the parlor were open; his studio was filled with tubes of paint, brushes and easels, blank canvases and paintings set out to dry. The scent of chemicals tore at his nostrils. The apartment was enormous; the location was perfect. The neighbors are hard-of-hearing pensioners, Einar had told him on one of his first visits, and they love me.

Hermann had told Einar about his date at five o'clock.

"Aha," Einar said, blowing smoke rings into the air. "With the young Ilse Stern, I presume?"

Hermann nodded.

"Yes," he said, slipping his hand into his jacket pocket to check that he had brought the tickets.

Why had he done it, bought those tickets? He'd been struck with the idea quite suddenly, hadn't given himself the chance to change his mind, had simply turned up at the box office and paid. Ilse so wanted to go to the pictures, as did he; he really just wanted to sit down, to disappear into something that had nothing to do with himself. Now the tickets are tucked inside the same jacket pocket, untouched, and he has a problematic explanation on his hands. He is nervous. He can't get mixed up in anything else, not now, he has enough on his plate. He can't allow somebody to get close to him, he's too anxious for that, it would only give him more to keep track of, too many loose threads, too many drawers in the nightmarish bureau that have to remain firmly locked. Things had been so good that summer, he and Ilse out in the backyard. But now, now it is autumn and everything has changed. It won't work, not now, he has enough to keep on top of. More than enough, really.

He can't help but imagine how Ilse will react when he sees her next. He closes his eyes and once again he pictures her, her dark hair, her neck, her body, her little snub nose that he's so fond of. She'll be angry with him and he'll have to take it, as usual, like a pig to the slaughter. He turns over, pulls the bedcovers over his head and hears the sound of his own breathing, short and irregular. He had never anticipated that it would be this tiring to keep on top of everything when they had asked him to be a part of things; he had imagined it all with such clarity, he had been so incredibly angry. Now he longs to renounce his role as the unreliable, inconsiderate boozer and aspiring artist. All he needs is one bloody drawer, just one, one drawer that can remain open regardless of who he is with. Deep within his heart he feels tired of being Hermann Rød. And tomorrow it all continues. The same again the day after that, and the day after that. But for how long, he wonders as he lies with his face turned to the wall, for how long can it really be worth it?

E VERYTHING IS WHITE.

Ilse isn't wearing any shoes. She is up to her knees in snow, standing in nothing but her nightdress; she can feel the cold wind as it rushes through the flimsy material, hitting her body like tiny, sharp pins. She can see the others; soft and blurred, vague figures in the white landscape, wrapped up well against the weather. Mum, Dad, Sonja, and Miriam. She calls out to them, tells them to stop, to wait for her. They can't hear her, they don't turn around. They continue to walk away from her, toward a faint, yellowish light that looks like a fire in the process of dying. She watches them walk away, until she can no longer see them and they vanish into a thick, steamy smog.

"Ilse?"

A voice. There, from deep within the snow. Slowly it makes its way through the cold air, through the snow and the ice and the smog and all the way to her ear, warm and pleasant. She lies there for a few seconds with her eyes closed as Miriam repeats her name.

She starts to pick up on other sounds: the clatter of metal and aluminum in the kitchen sink, her mother's quick, hardworking hands juggling saucepans, the sloshing of the water. Her father whistles a melody from the living room, she's heard it before, what is it called? The ticktock of the alarm clock on the bedside table, the tram outside the window, and the acute, high-pitched screech of the tracks; they must have opened the window slightly, it all seems louder than usual. Sound carries from the Rustads' apartment on the fourth floor: Karin and Lilly arguing, one of them crying, another shouting. Everything is so much louder when she lies with her eyes closed like this. Everything seems so fine and delicate, so easily broken.

"Ilse?" Miriam's face is at the edge of the bed. "Why did you shout?"

She's sitting on the floor with a sheet of paper in her lap and colored pencils scattered by her side: red, green, yellow.

"Did I shout?"

"Yes."

Ilse sits up in bed; she can feel a prickling sensation in her arm, she must have slept with it beneath her head at a strange angle. She gives it a little shake as if to bring it back to life once again and feels the way that the blood streams back to the affected area, tingling as it makes its way to each finger.

"What did I say?"

Miriam looks at her, curious. It's usually Sonja who talks in her sleep, mumbling words into the darkness; Ilse and Miriam are often woken up by her.

"I don't want to be alone."

Miriam's eyes are large and filled with questions.

"Did I really say that?"

"Mhm," Miriam replies. "And then you made a face like this." She screws up her face and makes a little round shape with her mouth. "Why did you say that, Ilse?"

Ilse has to think for a moment. What was it that she had been dreaming about? She closes her eyes to help her remember. The snow has disappeared. She is wearing her nightdress but she is warm beneath her covers, at home in her own bed. The others haven't vanished into a hazy smog. They're here, all at home in their apartment. It's a Sunday like any other. The usual sounds resonate throughout the rooms; the usual smells fill the air. Ilse tells Miriam about her dream, her eyes still tightly closed.

"But there's no snow now, Ilse. The sun is shining, look."

Their mother enters the room. She pauses in the doorway with her arms folded, standing there for a moment without uttering a word. Her green apron is knotted tightly around her waist, her hair in rollers under a thin hairnet, just like any other Sunday.

"I don't like it when you stay out so late, Ilse."

Here we go again, God! She had apologized to her mother when she came in yesterday evening, sorry again and again and again, she had allowed her mother to harp on until she had run out of words, and not once had she retorted with a single hurtful word of her own. When Ilse had let herself in, her mother had been sitting at the kitchen table, bolt upright in her chair. Then came the words, a barrage of them, like small bullets fired from a revolver. She should be more considerate. She was a member of this family too, and there were rules, and those rules applied to everyone. She was no exception. Ilse had said that she was sorry, that it wouldn't happen again. Her mother had calmed down eventually, and before she had gone to bed she had lifted a hand to Ilse's face and stroked her cheek. But now she was at it again, it was clear that she wasn't quite done.

"I didn't do it on purpose," Ilse mumbles.

"You never do, do you? And yet it's hardly a rare occurrence!"

Her mother whips off her hairnet in one swift wave and begins to unfurl the hair wrapped around one of the rollers. There's something about her straight-faced expression, an extra crease at the corners of her mouth. Her nimble fingers set to work teasing out roller after roller, each of which she places in the pocket of her apron as she huffs and puffs through tightly pursed lips.

"You don't know what it's like for us, Ilse. We worry about you. Your father even went over to ask the neighbor if he knew where you were."

Ilse sits up. She hadn't mentioned that part yesterday.

"The neighbor?"

"Yes," her mother continues, "we thought that you might have been with Hermann."

"And?"

"They had no idea where Hermann was either. He hadn't been home all day."

Her mother stands where she is for a few moments and looks at Ilse, pryingly, fishing for answers, nosier than ever. She finishes unrolling her curls; her hair is filled with soft brown clumps, like slugs forced to line up in formation, one after the next.

"I wasn't with Hermann," Ilse mumbles. Unfortunately, she wants to add.

Her mother pulls a comb from her apron pocket and begins to tackle the small slugs, unpicking each of them until her hair eventually resembles a soft, dark cloud around her head. She starts at the top once again, combing with regular swipes until her hair sits properly in place, the waves framing her slim face.

"Promise me that you won't ever come home that late again," she says.

"I won't, Mum. I promise."

Her mother lingers for a moment longer, casting her eyes around the room as if looking for something. The polka dot dress that Ilse had been wearing yesterday lies in a crumpled heap on the floor at the end of the bed. If her mother spots it now she'll ask questions.

"We're going out now," Mum says. "It's a beautiful day and we thought we'd take a walk. It's up to you if you want to come with us, but if you don't you can stay here for the next few hours and tidy your room. It's a mess in here, and most of that mess is yours."

She glances in the direction of the dress once again but obviously doesn't see it, because she leaves the room.

Ilse sits in her bed, taking a moment to think. What she really wants is some time to herself. She is never alone, the others are always there, never far from her presence, Mum and Dad, Sonja and Miriam, constantly around. She thinks back to her dream, how afraid she had been that they had left her, how alone she had felt, but it was just a dream, that's all, she'll stay at home and have some time to herself, do a little tidying. She has a lot to think about today, and a lot to clear up. She feels a sense of unease creeping through her; she's almost nauseous. It feels as if there's something lodged beneath her diaphragm and it aches.

Ilse glances at the clock on her bedside table. It's almost ten. She can't ever remember her family simply leaving her to sleep like that. They must have eaten breakfast without her, made their plans for the day, Mum might already even have prepared their dinner, and for a moment it feels as if they've lived a whole life during those quiet morning hours, no place for Ilse to join them.

She can hear her father in the living room, still sitting in his armchair by the window. He's started to sing now, the words to the same tune he was whistling before. "I was only eighteen when you first met me, the moon laughed and we danced to the most elegant melody." Ilse has a sudden urge to run and embrace him, to be three years old again and to clamber onto his lap, to sing along with him or simply sit quietly, imploring him to lift her high up in the air where she can kick her legs while safely held in his strong arms.

She makes her way into the living room.

"I'm not coming out today."

"Are you sure?" her father says. "We can wait for you. We're only going out to feel the autumn air."

Goodness, he really must be in a good mood; it is rare to hear him say such things, "out to feel the autumn air." Perhaps she should tag along, if only just to experience this side of her father, so different from the side of his character that they've seen of late. But she's made up her mind, there's far too much buzzing around inside her head, too much gnawing away at her, aching. Too many thoughts crisscross in her mind and she longs to sit quietly and work through each of them, one by one.

"I'm staying here."

She sits in the armchair after the others leave. The window is open just a crack and the light autumn breeze drifts in through the narrow gap, fresh and cool. A ripple of sound is carried in from the outside world: the tram trundling up Vogts gate, the shrill *brrring brrring* of a bicycle bell, then the sounds of another tram, this time making its way down the street, the bristling of someone sweeping the pavement, a plaintive cry for a mother's attention.

The view from the window is beautiful. Ekeberg Hill is red and yellow with autumn; in the bay at Bjørvika there are several boats drifting, large vessels too; and she can see the tenement buildings down in Grünerløkka, tiles and chimneys, the dusty square where all the brewery wagons line up one after the other, resting in the Sunday sunshine. If she could paint like Hermann, she would paint a picture of exactly what she can see today. Ugh, she's not supposed to be thinking about Hermann.

The apartment is so empty without the others. The door to the hallway is ajar; over in the corner in front of the window is the deep brown wooden dining table, surrounded by five chairs, and decked out in a yellow tablecloth adorned with her mother's neat embroidery and the brass candlestick with seven arms. Two coffee cups have been left sitting on the table from breakfast. The divan is on the other side of the living room, pushed up against the wall that divides the living room with the room she shares with her sisters. It's light brown, almost gray, and several patches have worn so thin that the stuffing has become visible. Mum and Dad pull it out every evening and push it back together again each morning.

Ilse observes the way that the sunlight creates strips of light throughout the room; she sees the dust particles that float in the air, hovering to create two dense pillars. She sees Miriam's clothing draped over a chair in the bedroom, a pair of tights rolled up by the wardrobe. Everything around her looks so peaceful, as if it's all meant to be exactly where it is at this moment in time.

There is a sheet of paper on the floor under the table. Ilse picks it up and turns it over to find one of Miriam's drawings. Five skinny stick people are depicted in cheerful colors, a large, childish sun above them, sunbeams so long that they cover the entire page. Dad is wearing a black hat, Mum is wearing a green skirt. In the bottom corner is a small figure with yellow hair; it must be Bella, Miriam's doll. In the opposite corner

Miriam has written her name in lopsided letters, followed by the date, the fourth of October 1942, written in Sonja's handwriting. Miriam must have drawn it earlier that day. It looks so idyllic, one happy family under a large yellow sun, everyone smiling. Yet everything is so very different.

Her own situation, for example. Does she have any reason to smile? Not today. Yesterday, perhaps. It's like that at your age, her mother would say, you'll grow out of it. But Ilse has a feeling that Mum is wrong about that, and that this won't be the kind of thing that she will grow out of. There is always more of everything with Ilse: more tears, more laughter, more commotion of all kinds. Had Mum been like that when she was fifteen? Ilse can't picture it, as hard as she may try.

Since the school term had ended, Ilse had been working for her father. Just until I figure out what I want to do, she had told him when she asked to work in the shop for a few months. The premises on Osterhaus' gate were small and cramped, a third-generation family business. Her father had worked there forever, it seemed, having become a trained tailor just like his own father and his father before him, and no doubt numerous other fathers before them. A few years ago things had been going well, with several employees and lots to keep him busy, but now, what with the war, everything had changed.

These were quiet days. Dad would sit and lightly drum his fingers against the countertop, the hands on the clock above the door crawling around the face at a snail's pace. She and Sonja and their father would eat lunch together without ever saying very much. The long, quiet hours suited Ilse perfectly. She was able to sit and read or chat with Sonja; it wasn't exactly the hardest job in the world. Mum and Dad wanted her to continue at school, they never stopped nagging her about it, and up until her final year she had been doing well. They had reluctantly agreed to let her take a year out to think about things; perhaps a year would give her time to mature, perhaps things would get back to normal again. It's this war, they would always say, exchanging grave expressions. It's all down to this war.

Sagene School was taken over by German soldiers, the schoolyard crammed with military equipment. Teaching had taken place here and there, in local buildings, in a church where they'd often sat freezing with no firewood; they'd even been taught in each other's homes on occasion. It was said that several of the teachers had been arrested and sent to work camps in the north, but it was impossible to keep track, one day they might hear one thing and the next day something else altogether; eventually Ilse had lost interest. She could just as well sit in the back room of the shop, sleepily daydreaming and secretly reading romantic novels.

She glances at the stick person with the black hat meant to represent her father. He's said so little lately, and though he smiles he doesn't look happy. The worry line on his forehead has expanded and deepened; now it looks like a straight line that divides his forehead in two. The choice of stock available to them is miserable, everything is rationed, and several of their regular customers have stopped coming to the shop.

"Is it because we're Jewish?" she had asked him one evening as the family was sitting around the dining table.

Her father didn't say anything. He pushed his chair back from the table, stood up, and disappeared into the kitchen.

This had happened several times lately, her father leaving the table in the middle of a meal without warning—he had stolen away, closed the door, they could all hear his footsteps going down the stairs. They always remained where they were, she and Sonja, Miriam and Mum, their gazes fixed on the tabletop as if they were ashamed somehow. He has a lot on his mind, Mum would say. Always the same old expressions. Poor Dad. Things aren't going well these days. Be nice to your father. Don't bother your father. It was like one long chorus of orders and embargoes, so many subjects that weren't supposed to be brought up. Dad had been like this for a while now. It had enveloped the family, descending on the apartment like a heavy blanket that was difficult to shake off. But today he had been happy, he was going out to feel the autumn air, he'd even given her a hug before he had left.

In Miriam's drawing, Mum has two black dots for eyes and a large red mouth in the shape of a wide smile. Maybe that's how Miriam sees her. Ilse has a different image of her. She can't recall the last time that she heard her mother laugh. She might chuckle slightly, or squeeze out a hoarse chortle, but laughter, real, proper, thigh-slapping guffaws that seem to erupt involuntarily, when was the last time that she'd heard that? When she closed her eyes and thought of her mother, she saw her leaning over a saucepan, mending holes in their clothing, scrubbing the floorboards on all fours, standing in long lines wearing a tense expression as she waited to receive their rations of sugar and coffee, flour and herring. And the whispering, that had increased in recent months, the irritating, dry sounds that escaped her lips, muttering, the words almost inaudible, a mumbling with no beginning and no end.

That was Mum. But there was something else too, something that Ilse had noticed lately. She would catch her mother standing and staring out the windows — she could remain there for so long that she resembled a statue concealed by the curtains, stock still and gazing outward, as if there were a better life out there, a life that could be hers if she could only stare at it for long enough.

Only one of the two medium-sized stick figures has been given any hair, long, brown lines that extend to the hips; it must be Sonja. The other figure has a few tufts sticking up from a round head. Ilse is afraid that it's supposed to be her.

Sonja will soon be nineteen years old, and she is Dad's right-hand woman in the shop and Mum's extra pair of hands at home. She learned to sew and is set to inherit the shop when Dad can't manage anymore. Sometimes Ilse thinks that if Sonja hadn't been quite so very good, she herself might have turned out better. If Sonja weren't so smart, perhaps she would have been smarter. Ilse couldn't be any of the things that Sonja was, so Ilse had taken on another role. She was the impulsive, thoughtless, joyful, irresponsible, childish member of the family. She had always been that way, there was no doubt about it. Occasionally Ilse felt a stab of envy when she saw her mother and Sonja sitting together at the kitchen table with their needlework in the evening, all while she lounged around with her nose stuck in a book. She had never been interested in knitting or sewing, any attempts always turned out lopsided and strange-looking and she was inevitably forced to unravel her yarn and unpick her stitches. Sonja executed everything she did with expert precision. Dad was lucky to have her.

The sun was large and yellow; why couldn't it be like it was in Miriam's drawing? Why couldn't it just hang from the ceiling in a corner of the apartment—brighten the place up a little? Things always used to be so good at home. On Fridays Mum would lay the table with a white cloth and bless the candles, then they'd eat and laugh together. Now it's as if they have to permanently monitor their actions to avoid saying anything wrong. Everything had changed so much over the past few months.

No, it must be herself that Miriam had drawn; she's the only one in the family who knows how to really, properly smile and laugh nowadays. She spent her days at home with her colored pencils, playing with Karin from the fourth floor, a simple, charmed life. It must be nice to be five and a half years old.

It's so quiet without the others around, the only sound Ilse can hear is the alarm clock in the bedroom as the lazy ticking reverberates throughout the apartment. No, there's something else too, the sound of someone crying. It's coming from the fourth floor; it must be Karin. Ilse can hear Mrs. Rustad hushing her and the sound of a child's voice calling "Daddy."

The walls are so thin here. In the evenings, she and Sonja can hear Mr. and Mrs. Rustad in the bedroom above their own, every word they say, every sound they make; it's as if the two of them have crept in and hidden under the couple's marital bed. They have the same apartment layout, two rooms and a kitchen, but on the floor above, it is the parents who sleep in the bedroom while their two daughters share a bunk bed in one corner of the living room. Ilse and Sonja are always extra attentive when they hear the sound of creaking from the bed, slow and deliberate to begin with, gradually increasing in pace, faster and faster before silence falls once again.

She looks out the window, where she can see Ole Rustad parking his taxi outside the front of the building. He removes his cap when he catches sight of her, bowing deeply before smiling and waving up at her.

For a split second she finds herself wondering whether Hermann has come home, whether he's sitting in the apartment next door; perhaps he's thinking of her too. A new thought arises, why hasn't it occurred to her before? What if he'd taken somebody else with him to the pictures instead? What if he had sat next to another girl in row seven, seats eight and nine? A girl with fair hair and pale eyes, soft curves, large breasts, a slim waist. All of a sudden she can imagine it, the two of them snuggled up close. The girl probably had a nice name too, something like Cordelia or Henriette. She might have leaned in close to him and whispered how happy she was to have been invited to the pictures, and maybe Hermann would have told her that he had actually asked someone else first, just to make himself appear more interesting. But who? the girl might ask him, and what would Hermann have said to that? Just the girl next door. Her name's Ilse; I know, it's a strange name, isn't it? And then the girl might have asked what this Ilse looked like, and Hermann would have shrugged his shoulders and said, well, she's fine, not that ugly and not that beautiful either.

She stops herself, then stands before the mirror that hangs between the two living room windows.

"This is me," she announces to her reflection. She smiles to herself for a moment, a strained, forced expression that quickly evaporates. "Unfortunately," she adds.

It's no wonder that Hermann didn't want to go to the pictures with her, not really, she can see that now. She's just started reading a new book, and a very interesting one at that. She remembers a sentence that had stuck with her: "First and foremost, a woman must become well-acquainted with her own appearance, and then she must know how she *wants* to appear to the world." This has to be exactly the right time and place for such a study, alone in the apartment with a few hours to herself before the others will return home. Ilse enters the bedroom, fetches her notebook from the bedside table, and takes it into the living room.

"Comments I have received about my appearance," she writes. On second thought she squeezes in the word "Positive" in smaller handwriting at the start of the swiftly scrawled heading. She sits and ponders, unable to think of anything at all, not a single word. Dad says that she is his beautiful girl, but that doesn't count. He's her father, of course he would say that.

What was it that Hermann had said not so long ago? That she looked like a little squirrel? He had smiled as he had said it, she remembers it so clearly, she even remembers where they had been standing, out in the backyard; it was summertime, the last day of July. It must have been a compliment of sorts. Can she add that one to the list? Squirrels are cute, small, soft, and sweet. She writes "resembles a squirrel," and in brackets adds "Hermann," just to make clear from whom the compliment came. She thinks some more. That can't be the only one. A squirrel. Is that all she has to write? This is stupid.

Recently she has slipped something new into her evening prayers. First she covers the usual, thank you for everything I have, watch over the people I care about, don't let anything bad happen to anyone, always recited swiftly and in no particular order, mostly just so that it has been said, just to be on the safe side. But then she gets to the heart of the matter, the important part that is a message exclusively shared between Ilse and God: Dear, good, kind Lord, I don't mean to bother you but please help me, I need to be beautiful. Ilse Stern needs to be more beautiful!

She stands up, takes off her clothes, and starts at her feet, studying them for a moment before leaning over the table and writing: "Big toe on left foot is at a strange angle. Everything else fine." It annoys her that one toe has to be that way, veering to the left, almost witchlike.

Her legs. They're slim, but her skin is dry. She wets a finger in her mouth and draws it along her leg; it creates a stripe in a different color, fresher looking, no longer quite so white. Might butter help? Mum would be furious if she were to apply butter to her legs; if there was anything her mother had any control over it was the tiny knob of butter they managed to buy when there was any to be had at the shop. She recalls the flour episode, how she had patted it on her face to see if it could be used as powder; she'd taken so little but there had been such a kerfuffle about it, it would only be worse if she were to touch the butter.

Her thighs don't meet in the middle. There's a gap between them when she stands with her lower legs touching. She thinks of Sonja as she makes her notes. When Sonja undressed in the evenings, Ilse would compare their bodies. Sonja's irritatingly tiny waist formed a slim meeting point between her upper and lower body, her breasts perfectly round, the muscles in her back visible when she bent over to pull off her tights. She looked like a sculpture in a museum, Ilse mused. No such luck for her, though; she was like an unsuccessful early attempt concealed within the sculptor's workroom, deep in a cellar, a model carved in stone that refused to be manipulated into something more appealing, sharp and strange and utterly impossible to put on display.

Her breasts. What a sad, sorry mess. Sonja had started wearing a proper bra when she had turned fourteen, the kind that fastened at the back with three catches. Sonja hoisted and squeezed and hooked things into their proper place while Ilse stood beside her in a childish undershirt. She had asked their mother if she could have one too, the kind with hooks at the back. One day during the winter her mother had come home with a parcel for her; she had been to the lingerie shop, but she had bought a different type, one without hooks. It was a tight undershirt that had to be pulled over your head and which neither lifted nor hitched up anything in the slightest.

Maybe she could put something inside her undershirt, socks or some of her mother's yarn, two small balls, maybe? She notes the idea down in her book, something she can return to at a later date. Imagine if Miriam turned out like Sonja; she suddenly pictures them both as adults. Two sisters with finely sculpted bodies, breasts like ripe fruit, and then Ilse, all sharp lines in an undershirt stuffed with itchy balls of yarn. Ugh, it doesn't bear thinking about.

At least I'm happy with my ears, she thinks, turning her head from side to side in front of the mirror. They're neat and a nice shape and don't stick out from her head. She is almost tempted to write "pretty ears" in her notebook. She smiles to herself. Ilse with the pretty ears. It's something, and a little something at that, but better than nothing at all.

Her dark hair is shoulder length when she undoes her braids. She shakes her head and hopes that it might form pretty waves; she's had her braids in for a good long while now. It doesn't sit prettily, not at all. It looks untidy and wispy, dangling down like dry straw. She inspects strands of hair, pinching them between her thumb and forefinger, observing the split ends. When it comes down to it, her hair is the only thing that she can realistically do anything about, and she needn't delay the task. It's almost as if the scissors are sitting primed and ready for her in the kitchen drawer. Positioned in front of the living room mirror, she tries to work out exactly how much to trim. Not too much; she has to try and get it just right. She opens the scissors and lets her hair fill the gap between the blades before squeezing tight and watching as the clipped hair floats to the floor. She cuts it to the same length all the way around, but when she's finished she notices that it's shorter on the left-hand side, lopsided. She snips at the right-hand side a little, finds her pocket mirror, and checks the back of her head. Is it still uneven? She snips a little more, then a little more after that. Now it's quite short, the ends tickling the middle of her neck. Will she be able to tie it up anymore? She tries pulling it back, but the hair at the sides is too short and slips out of her grasp.

Ilse quickly gathers up the tufts of hair on the floor and throws them into the rubbish bin in the kitchen. Why did she have to do that today? Couldn't she have made better use of this miserable day by doing some-thing more constructive than taking stock of her own appearance? Now her stomach aches even more than it did before; the sense of discomfort has somehow expanded, a creeping queasiness that seems to flutter within her. She's tempted to march over and knock on

Hermann's front door, just to gain even the slightest smidgen of comfort.

"But that's the last thing you're going to do," she chides herself. From here on in *he'll* have to seek *her* out. If Hermann happens to bump into Ilse with the pretty ears, *he'll* be the one making all of the effort.

ONJA SITS HUNCHED OVER THE SEWING machine with one foot resting on the pedal, her elbows on the table; she fiddles with a pencil, sketching on a piece of paper and pretending to work. The clock above the front door tells her it's fifteen minutes past closing time. Darkness is beginning to set in; there's a faint gray tinge to the evening air outside, almost like fog.

Her father is sweeping the floor. He whistles softly, swaying slightly on his feet with each long, meticulous stroke of the broom, the swishing sound of the bristles resonating in the space. Ilse sits farther inside the shop reading, apparently entirely absorbed by her book.

They should both surely be heading home soon, Sonja thinks to herself. They usually leave as soon as Dad has locked the door and flipped the sign that hangs in the window. Ilse has a habit of pacing impatiently, sometimes as early as half an hour before closing time, glancing at the clock, sighing and hurriedly gathering her things as if she can't leave quickly enough.

Sonja drums two fingers against the tabletop, making small, nervous gestures and glancing toward the back room. Nobody suspects a thing, nobody has noticed that anything is missing, nobody has asked why she has been staying behind recently after the others have left. Don't wear yourself out, my girl, her father has said, gazing upon her with a mixture of pride and unease. She was his eldest daughter, and here she was, sacrificing her own time for the sake of the family business, staying behind at work in the evenings, giving everything she had to help keep things afloat. If only he knew.

"Ilse?" Sonja almost whispers. "Ilse, it's quarter past."

Ilse looks up at Sonja for a moment, casting a glance at the clock before looking back down at her book.

"I just have to finish this chapter," she mumbles.

Her father sets aside his broom, leaning it against the wall in a corner of the room. He picks up the dustpan and throws the sweepings into the dustbin.

"No," he says, clasping his hands together in front of him. "Your mother will be waiting for us at home."

He makes his way into the back room, fetching his coat and putting on his hat before looking at them both with surprise.

"Aren't you coming, girls?" he asks.

Sonja inserts a needle in the machine, her hands fumbling as if she were a novice—she's done this hundreds of times, thousands even, but at this moment it is as if her brain can't send the necessary signals to her fingers quite quickly enough.

"I'll stay a little longer, Dad," she says without looking up at him.

"Again?" he asks. "You need to eat, Sonja. Surely there's nothing with such an urgent deadline?"

Sonja wets the dark blue cotton between her lips and threads it through the eye of the needle.

"I'm just finishing up Mrs. Nagel's order," she says, her voice low. "You two go on, I won't be long."

"This is unbelievable!" Ilse exclaims, slapping her book closed. "I can't believe I haven't read this before. It's as if it's been written about *me*; I mean, there's even an annoyingly pretty older sister." Ilse flashes Sonja half a smile.

They both eventually leave. Sonja waits for a few minutes before moving; if her father had forgotten something, he could come back to fetch it.

The shop is quiet. Sonja makes her way toward the back room. The box is there, under a table. She slides it out and removes the lid, reaching inside and feeling the cool, thin fabric in her hands. She carries the item over to the sewing table, unfolding it and standing for a moment to observe it. There's not much left to do, just sewing the edging and removing the tacking thread; she

might even finish this evening if she works quickly. She's
due to deliver it on Tuesday, only a few days from now.

For several years now, Sonja has visited the National
Theater, sneaking in after the performances have begun,
content to stand until her feet ache in the darkness of
the auditorium, gazing upon the costumes on display.
Dresses that sparkle in the stage lights, hats, wigs,
high-heeled shoes that click-clack across the stage, a
world of perfume and heavy tapestries, applause and
chandeliers, highly strung actresses and well-to-do
people sipping from tiny glasses during intermissions.
More recently she's taken a notebook with her to make
sketches, her head full of dreams, troublesome, beautiful. It went against everything that she was, everything
that was intended for her, everything that had been decided for her from the start.

Only a month ago she had bumped into Helene
from her sewing course. Sonja had been looking at
the posters framed behind glass outside the theater,
reading about the next performance, *Mary Stuart*,
another play she longed to see.

"Sonja?"

She looked up. Helene stood before her, smiling in a
brown coat fitted at the waist. She had just left work,
she said, nodding at the large theater building.

"You work in the theater?" Sonja replied, astonished.

"I've been here for a while now," Helene said. "I work in the sewing room. It's good fun, and they pay quite well too. I've moved into my own little place, a room with a kitchen in Majorstua. What about you?"

Sonja told Helene she was working in her father's shop.

"They need more seamstresses here," Helene said. "I could recommend you, I know how good you are. Imagine if we worked here together! That would be wonderful. But you have to submit a sample costume, and you need to supply your own fabric for it. Do you have anything in the shop you could use?"

Sonja pictured the back room of the shop. It wasn't exactly overflowing with materials, and they hadn't had any nice fabrics for a long time, mostly just coarse wool and thick tweed for stitching hard-wearing coats.

"I'm sure I can get my hands on something," she said, still unsure of how in the world she'd go about it.

Later that evening Sonja had gone through the shop, upending boxes, rifling through drawers, hunting through the contents of shelves and turning the storeroom upside down; there had to be something that she could use, something that her father had stashed away and forgotten about. Inside a box tucked away deep within the storeroom she had found a thin white material, crumpled and carrying the faint smell of mildew, but Sonja had carefully lifted it from where it had been stowed away, feeling the quality of the fabric and admiring the way it draped in her hands. She settled herself at her sewing table and began sketching. What did they want to see? It would need to be something magnificent, something impressive that would look good onstage.

Sonja unfolds the dress that she has tacked together. It might not be a costume, as such—it isn't particularly resplendent, impressive, sparkling, or voluminous, and it certainly isn't worthy of being donned by a diva on the stage. Nonetheless, it is good handiwork; surely they'll be able to see that. The dress itself is sewn in the fine, almost transparent material, which she lined with thicker, more rigid inner fabric. Nipped in at the waist, the skirt cascades in one soft, smooth wave, and she plans to add a trim to the plunging neckline using a small piece of silk that she found lying around. The smell continues to linger, a nauseating odor of mildew, dust, and darkness.

Her father hasn't noticed. Not yet. What if he were to find out that she has been slinking around after closing time like a thief in the night, making plans a world away from those he has for her? Her stomach has ached at the mere thought of it. And if her sample is successful, if the theater were to employ her? Her parents would be so disappointed; her father paid for her sewing course, it had been expensive but it was an investment, in the business, in Sonja, and ultimately something that would benefit him too. She would take over, run the business in the future, but had he ever even asked her if that's what she wanted? When had they ever had that conversation?

Sonja has always wanted to sew, she's always liked working with her hands, creating something beautiful or practical, taking a length of material and transforming it into something new. Dresses lighter than air. Suits in soft, comfortable fabric. Coats with fur collars. Tailoring for men. Drawing sketches, making patterns, snipping and tacking, she could make anything she wanted to—she was skilled, her hands were steady, her approach was methodical, she was like a magician drawing new items of clothing from her hat with nothing but the wave of a wand. But here, what could she create here in the long run? Could she really remain in her father's dusty premises, mending other people's clothing, taking in and letting out, sitting in the dimly lit shop and watching the passing of the sun through the shop windows?

At home they're used to the fact that Sonja clears the table once they've eaten. Sonja does the washing up, Sonja darns the socks, Sonja knits and sews, Sonja hangs the laundry out to dry in the backyard. Sonja or Mum, rarely ever Ilse. Her mother nagged Ilse, running around after her and asking her to tidy up, sending her to the shop with a list, scolding her. Ilse would shout right back, ugh, you never stop, she would say, sullen. Mum tried to teach Ilse needlecraft, Sonja even had a go, but to no avail. I can't do it, Ilse would cry, casting her work away, the needles clattering against each other, I'm sorry but it's just not for me. Sonja was thirteen when Miriam was born. She had changed her and cared for her, fed her, rocked her to sleep in the evenings, knitted her clothing. Ilse was only nine at the time, but would things have been any different if it had been Ilse who had been thirteen instead? Would she have done the things that Sonja had done, would she have been given the same responsibilities? Ilse was an older sister too, but it was different, she played with Miriam, drew with her, took her for walks around the block, showed her the world. Sonja waited at home with dishcloths and dressing-downs, head lice comb in one hand and cod-liver oil in the other.

Ilse dreamed of traveling abroad. She even said the word in her own special way, abroaaaad, she would say, when I grow up I'm going to travel abroaaaad. She talked about America, Paris. Sonja's greatest desire was to have a profession that would satisfy her, to earn her own money, move away from home, rent a little place of her own.

At home Ilse tells stories; her laughter is contagious and spreads with such ease, and she can do uncanny impressions of their neighbors. She makes such a fuss if there is something wrong, loud enough that everyone can hear, but Sonja buries her face into her pillow when something troubles her, turning to look at the wall, silent and invisible tears melting into the pillow. The nights are teeming with dreams; distinct, tingling, quivering, like a swarm of bees. Over the course of the past few weeks her dreams have woken her almost every night, causing her to sit up in bed, suddenly aware of the sweat across her chest, her nightdress damp and clinging to her body, the sense of unease that streams into the darkness, the regularity of her sisters' breathing, her mother and father too, both asleep in the next room, entirely unaware of Sonja's plans.

Sonja removes the pins from the trim, smoothing out the fabric and carefully slipping it into place in the machine. She puts a little pressure on the foot pedal and hears the recognizable hum of the machine in action. If she were to work at the theater, she'd be bringing more money in, she could contribute more at home. Perhaps she could put it to them like that; after all, Helene *had* said it was well-paid work, perhaps Mum and Dad would accept that, she'd adopt the role that she'd always assumed, the one that she was used to, the one that they wanted her to have. At the same time she remembered what Helene had said about renting a place to live. A room with a kitchen in the city center. Imagine that! Sonja can already recite the advertisement she'd place: "Young woman in permanent employment seeking furnished room for rent." She'd seen many others like it in the newspapers. It was probably more expensive to rent a furnished room, but she didn't own anything, not even a single chair, so furnished it would have to be. She has pictured it so many times, the same scene: leaving the theater late one evening having worked all that day, wandering through the Royal Palace Park in the cool night air and unlocking the door to her own home. She can see the furnished room as clear as day: a bed, a table and chair, her own clothes, all of her things, a room of her own where she can lock the door behind her, space to breathe. It didn't have to be in Majorstua, it could be anywhere at all. A door, a bed, a room. Peace and quiet.

The trim is in place, and now all that remains is to remove the tacking stitches. Sonja glances at the clock. It's late. She'll have to finish the rest after closing time tomorrow. She places the dress inside the box, putting on the lid and carrying it into the back room, then unhooking her coat from the peg, finding the keys, and opening the front door. The air is hazy and dense, heavy with autumn. She locks up the shop, and as she does so she catches sight of her reflection in the glass window-pane. In the frosted glass everything looks different: her head, body, face, gaze; it is as if the pieces don't quite fit together.

ISAK SITS ON THE EDGE OF HIS BED FOR A few moments before getting up. Hanna lies facing the wall. He can hear the sound of her breathing, quiet and steady. Over the past week he's been woken several times by her tossing and turning; the bed creaks beneath them and she talks in her sleep, mumbling, indistinct. And on those mornings that he has woken before her, he has lain in the darkness, alone and deep in thought. Now she rests in silence with her legs tucked up underneath her body. Gently he pulls the blanket up over her shoulders. It's only just past six o'clock; she can rest for another hour before she needs to be up and about.

The living room is dark; the door into the girls' room is closed. Isak gets dressed in the kitchen. He pulls aside the heavy curtain just enough to see what kind of day it will be. It looks cold, sparkling—he dreads the first snowfall, it's due any day now; he's never liked snow. His breakfast awaits him on the kitchen worktop, packed up and ready for him to take. He never eats at home before work, never feels much like eating in the mornings, never feels hungry. Hanna makes him something in the evenings and packs it up for him to eat at work, and it's not until then that he really feels like it. He slides his sandwich into his coat pocket, quickly glances at his reflection in the mirror, places his hat on his head, and quietly turns the latch.

There's something lying on the doormat. It's white, a piece of paper; he almost steps on it. He bends down and picks it up—it's an article, half a page ripped from a newspaper. The headline, the illustration, they seem to flash up at him. He stands for a moment with the paper in his hand, looking up and down the empty hallway.

"Hello?" he whispers.

Nobody answers. He places the piece of paper in his coat pocket and walks down the stairs.

The air is crisp today. He feels the quivering of his pulse as the blood rushes through his body. Will it creep into his home too, this torment, those words, will it be even remotely possible to find peace, to breathe, to live? Must he start each day by filling a bucket with soapy water and standing outside in the cold to hurriedly wipe down the glass windowpanes? He's started to get up even earlier than usual; every day he does his best to make sure that he is at the shop before the girls arrive, at least an hour in advance of them just in case there is anything to scrub from the windows. They shouldn't be forced to face that. He had felt a jolt of horror pass through him the first time it had happened: *Jewish scum brought the war to Norway 9 April*. The large white block capitals covered the entire shop window. It no longer instills the same fear in him as it had that first day. Nowadays he simply fetches the bucket, an automatic reaction, no thinking, just washing: *Jewish parasites*, he scrubs until the words disappear; a Star of David, he pours soap on the cloth, creates a lather, sometimes he has to use his nails, scrape the words from the glass.

Isak Stern tries to smile. He tries to be friendly. He tries to be the man he's always been. Hardly any customers visit the shop these days and his accounts are beginning to drift into the red; it's difficult to obtain stock, difficult to run an independent business. But Isak smiles, as often as he can. He may succeed only occasionally, he knows that, but he forces himself to be positive whenever Hanna asks him how he is doing; everything is just fine, he tells her. He can no longer look her in the eye when he does so.

He stands on Beier Bridge and watches the cascades of water that drum against the smooth stones in the Akerselva River. The leaves of the trees are red and yellow and there is a light breeze in the air around him; spray rises from the water, a damp, suffocating vapor. He reaches into his pocket, his hands freezing cold, pulling out the page torn from the newspaper. The cartoon shows a man with black hair and a pronounced nose, his hands grabbing at coins, his fingers long and crooked, greedy. *We are drowning in a flood of people who are a scourge on the communities in which they settle. Help us to stem the tide. Prevent our land from becoming Europe's rubbish heap.* The bridge trembles slightly beneath his feet as a man cycles past. Isak scrunches up the paper in his hand and casts it into the waterfall, watching as it is swallowed up by the frothing depths.

It could be the new family on the fourth floor. The Kjølbergs moved in just before the summer after Mrs. Nilsen passed away; mother, father, and a boy around ten years old. Isak has noticed how they look the other way whenever he passes. Hanna told him about one occasion when she and Mrs. Kjølberg had both been hanging washing on their respective clotheslines in the backyard. Her son had wandered over to Miriam and had started talking to her. Without a moment's hesitation his mother had been at his side, pulling him to her with a stern look while whispering: "They're Jewish, Finn, you mustn't talk to the likes of them." The situation had alarmed Hanna; imagine saying such a thing to a child, she had said. And what had Isak done when he heard? He had stroked Hanna's cheek and smiled. Imagine, he had said, feeling a wave of anger swelling within him, nausea rising in the pit of his stomach.

He feels the same sense of rage now, as he approaches the shop premises. He knows that today will require all the effort he can muster to plaster on a smile. The girls usually arrive at eight o'clock, which means he has an hour; an hour to eat his breakfast, prepare the day's orders, clean and tidy the shop floor, maybe polish the windows. An hour to calm himself down. And then, when the clock strikes eight, he won't think about how the day started, but will welcome his daughters with a smile and open the shop to customers. If there are to be any, that is.

He lets himself in, draws the curtains, and allows the bluish morning light to flood in through the windows that line the street outside. He sits on the stool behind the counter, motionless, staring into the room. It is as if everything crowds around him this morning, everything that he has worried about and tried to keep at bay, it all surges into the silent shop.

He knows that he's not alone. He knows other Jews with their own businesses in Oslo, and they all tell the same stories: customers who have stopped shopping with them, articles in the newspapers. It wasn't long ago that the sewing machines had blazed through long lists of orders in the back room. There had been no shortage of customers, and many an evening he'd stayed on at the shop to get everything finished in time. He'd had the money to pay several seamstresses, to pay himself a wage; he'd even paid to have a cleaner. And now, what was left of it all now? They could only just cover the essentials, he and Sonja and Ilse too, more recently. This wasn't what he wanted for them; in fact, it was nothing like it. They would receive a much better wage elsewhere, but he couldn't let them work for nothing. He had decided to try to pretend that things would be back to normal before long, though he couldn't do so indefinitely, and could barely sustain it as things stood. But the joy of having one's own money, even very little, yes, that was a joy that he wanted his girls to experience. He should have taught Sonja to keep the books, but if he had then it wouldn't have taken her long to realize that things weren't as they ought to be. She'd start to worry, he thought; really it was better to wait.

He had been struck with an idea in the summer and suddenly, without being able to explain why, he had found himself heading to the bank. There he had withdrawn every penny that he had successfully put aside before closing the account and taking his money home. He had also emptied the family's safety deposit box.

There wasn't much in there: a few items of jewelry that Hanna had inherited from her mother, some valuables that his own parents had passed on to him. He had placed everything in a cigarette tin and had hidden it in the chest of drawers under a pile of his folded underwear. He hadn't said a word to Hanna.

He sits and gently taps the fingers of one hand against his sandwich. A coffee would be nice, he thinks to himself, a steaming hot cup of coffee, the good stuff, a whole pot. All of a sudden he catches sight of a piece of paper lodged beneath Sonja's sewing machine, a sketch; it looks like the outline of a dress. His curiosity piqued, he gets up and walks over to Sonja's sewing station to take a closer look. He can't recall anyone having ordered such a garment, but it's possible that Sonja has taken on a project that she hasn't mentioned to him. The dress has an elegant trim and is tailored at the waist with a deep, plunging neckline. Quite old-fashioned, he thinks; it might be a new take on an older design, something the customer had found hidden away in a cupboard, perhaps. Sonja had stayed late at work over the past few evenings. He had noticed the way that she had often avoided meeting his gaze, somehow uneasy. He didn't doubt that she understood more about things than he liked to imagine. Maybe he ought to bring up the subject of bookkeeping with her soon after all, then; to admit defeat when the numbers spoke for themselves in black and white.

The anxiety, the vulnerability, they had crept up on him. It had all started with the wireless. They had been instructed to hand in their radio set before anyone else. He had lugged the heavy Tandberg apparatus out of the living room and had handed it over to the authorities. They weren't permitted to own a wireless, and soon the same could be said of the rest of the population too, but on that day, as he hauled the heavy wooden set around town, the order only applied to Jews. He had returned home to sit in the armchair by the window and the room had been silent; he could make out the faintest strains of music from the Rustads' apartment above them on the fourth floor, a lively melody, he knew the words, hummed along, stared at the shelf where their own wireless had been for the past few years, now no more than a gaping hole in the room. Hanna eventually moved a vase there, but whenever he caught the sound of music from the floor above, the silence of his own home overwhelmed him. In the end he dismantled the entire bookshelf, placing the pieces in storage in the building's cellar. Only the holes in the wall remain.

In the winter they had received word that their identification papers were to be stamped with a letter J. That same evening he had sat in his armchair after the others had gone to bed, his papers in his lap, staring at the fat red symbol that loomed like a talon by his photograph. A letter, something and nothing; he had felt so utterly powerless, they could just as well have stamped his forehead. Even then he'd had his suspicions that things could only get worse.

It didn't take long; only a few weeks later they had been required to fill in a form. He had turned up at the police station to fetch the papers and had faced a long list of questions: nationality, citizenship, private address, religious affiliation. Everyone over the age of fifteen whose papers had been stamped with a J needed to fill in three copies of the same document. Isak had placed the papers in a drawer at the shop; this wasn't the kind of thing that he wanted his daughters to worry about; maybe he could sort it out himself somehow, fill in the forms on their behalf. He practiced forging their signatures, Ilse's childish scribble, Sonja's soft script; he thought he might be able to make it work but Hanna had refused to allow him. They couldn't forge signatures, it was only a few documents, it would be fine for the girls to fill them in. The family had gathered around the table at home.

"What do I put for the last question?" Ilse had asked.

He read the two final sentences on the sheet of

paper. *When did you arrive in Norway? Previous country of residence outside of Norway?*

"Just leave it blank," he had mumbled.

He unwraps his sandwich and takes a bite of the brown bread, chewing for longer than necessary, thinking. He has heard stories. People who leave everything behind, their work, their homes, uproot themselves in every respect. Many of them have made it over to Sweden. It's one option. How would Hanna react to such a suggestion? Would she consider it, putting the girls through it; would *he*, for that matter? He doesn't know how to go about it, where to begin, who to contact. It's not the kind of thing that you can simply ask for more information about, not like a vacation where you identify your destination and hotel of choice. If he starts to look into this he has to know what he's doing, and by that point the decision has to have been made. He needs to think it through, properly evaluate the situation before he involves Hanna in his plans. He'll keep the girls out of it too, they shouldn't have to worry about this kind of thing, he can do this alone.

It's a sunny day, he can see that now. Bright light seeps in through the windows. He enters the back room and fetches the sign to be hung in the display window: *Do you have extra material at home? Your unwanted fabric can be transformed into a dress.* Just as he hangs the sign in the window, he sees Sonja and Ilse approaching. It must be eight o'clock. He closes his eyes for a moment, tries to picture something pleasant, thrusts any thorny thoughts aside. And then, when he opens his eyes again, there they are, the very image he had attempted to conjure up: his girls, Sonja and Ilse. He feels the strain as he forces a smile, his jaw muscles quivering.

"Good morning, girls," he says as they step inside.

I LSE WAITS OUTSIDE RINGNES BREWERY for the workers to head home for the day. Half hidden behind a tree, she doesn't want Hermann to see her, but she just *has* to see him today, to see if he looks different, to see if he goes home or not, and if not, to see where he does go.

Hermann hasn't been to see her. It has been silent. Deafeningly silent. Ilse has sat in the kitchen each evening with one ear pressed up against the wall, listening. Footsteps from inside the apartment, echoes from the stairwell, someone coming up the stairs, another walking down, doors opening and closing, voices. Bolt upright, she's held her breath with each sound, only to collapse once again when silence falls.

Hermann Rød. She has tried her best to force him from her thoughts: his smell, his body, his hair, his voice, his hands, she's tried to eradicate all trace of him, to lock it all away somewhere. But then there it is, yet again, spilling out without warning, oozing through the cracks like tiny, bitter droplets. She doesn't want to be some kind of lapdog, lying there barking, begging, scratching at his door. He should come to *her*, he should ask for *her* forgiveness, explain himself, row seven, seats eight and nine, she really needs to stop mulling over it all. It's been six days, seven, eight, fourteen now; the wait is agonizing.

During those first few days she spent all of her time reading, thinking about just how smart and pretty she'd make herself, figuring out how she wanted to look and following all the book's advice. Every evening she carefully applied Vaseline to her eyelids. On the first evening she had used far too much of the sticky salve and had spent at least half an hour in the kitchen with water and a washcloth, blinking erratically on account of the stinging sensation. She's better at it now, she just has to close her eyes and apply a thin layer before fumbling her way to the bedroom. Every morning she sits in the armchair and places a warm cloth over her face while the others set the table and prepare breakfast.

But there has been no word from Hermann Rød.

Eventually she catches sight of him, walking her way, sauntering along as he talks to a boy in a gray jacket who is pushing a bicycle, both of them laughing. She can hear him chuckling; what can he possibly find so funny at this exact moment in time, why is he in such a good mood? Ilse follows them, keeping her distance though never so far away that she risks losing sight of him. The boy with the bicycle disappears down Thorvald Meyers gate. Hermann continues toward Birkelunden Park and halts at the tram stop, where he stands and gazes vacantly out over the park, his smile having faded. When the tram pulls up he enters the first set of doors. Ilse sneaks in through the doors at the back. He stands in the middle of the tram, she can see his arm through the crowd of people, his wrist; he holds on tight to the loop that hangs from the arched ceiling and she can see the sleeve of his jacket sliding down his arm. The tram judders through the district of Grünerløkka as it approaches the city center. He's on his way to see the artist, he must be. Ilse doesn't know where the artist lives, she doesn't even know his name, but she can imagine him, an old man, tall, slim, dressed just so, with a mustache that curls up at the ends, slicked-back hair, and cloaked in strong cologne, ugh. Hermann has said so little about him. He told her that his lessons are in Frogner, and precious little else. I'm learning a lot, he told her, and nothing more. She's questioned him several times, come on Hermann, tell me what he looks like, the artist, tell me what he's teaching you—but he doesn't want to, he squirms his way out of conversation, turns away, clams up, scratches his cheek, smiles, and asks her about something else, anything else.

The tram pulls up at the stop by the National Theater. Two policemen board, both wearing dark uniforms, their voices booming as they force their way through the busy carriage. Ilse sees Hermann shake his head, lowering his gaze and hunching over then looking out the window before walking toward the conductor. Is he getting off? It looks like it. She makes her way toward the doors at the back of the carriage, waits for the tram to stop by Palace Park, readies herself to disembark, yes, he's getting off now. She hurriedly follows suit. Hermann continues along Drammensveien, following the tram tracks, moving quickly until he reaches Solli Square, heading in the same direction as the tram. He's walking so quickly, she hangs back and watches him cut diagonally across the street and head down Bygdøy allé, his back as he walks away, his shoes against the asphalt. The tall tenement buildings are lined up as straight as an arrow in the dwindling afternoon light; there's barely a soul to be seen. At a crossroad he turns right, glancing around him and hurrying along the pavement. He comes to a halt outside a door on the corner of a large white building; the street sign reads Frederik Stangs gate. He rings the top bell, stands outside for a moment, and then disappears through the door. It booms loudly as it closes behind him.

Ilse waits. Her breathing is shallow, rapid; her pulse thuds. She approaches the door. There is a small sign next to the top doorbell that reads "E. Vindju." She steps back and looks up at the fourth floor, the apartment on the right-hand side. An expansive window looks out onto the street and she can see a faint light emanating from within, more windows all in a row, all dark, and a curved, ornamental balcony protruding from the outer wall. How long do they usually spend up there? She could wait until he reappears outside, sneak back on the tram home behind him, or she could ring the bell, ask to speak to him, ask if he can come outside, or maybe even if she could go in. He's so close to her now, only a few floors up from where she stands, nothing separating them but a staircase, a few doors. And yet still he seems so far away. She traces her finger up the row of door-bells, all the stairs, the doors, all the pending explanations, revelations. The leaves along the street have gathered in small mounds, dry, yellow, red, rustling against the asphalt. She won't be a lapdog, she won't scratch at his door, she looks up and back down the street, then up at the window, the light still visible, then heads back in the direction of Bygdøy allé.

E INAR WAITS IN THE DOORWAY AS HERMANN climbs the stairs. He holds a glass in one hand and a cigarette in the other, a grave expression on his face; he doesn't smile when he catches sight of Hermann, not like usual. Hermann can feel the blood pumping through his veins. He had bounded up the stairs, taking three steps at a time as if he couldn't get over the threshold soon enough, couldn't close the door to Einar's apartment behind him with enough haste, couldn't wait to be there, inside, the door locked, invisible to the outside world.

The two policemen on the tram must have come from the police headquarters; the sight of their uniforms had made him feel sick and he'd started to sweat in the overcrowded carriage. He had overheard the sound of conversation behind him, a meter, two maybe, raucous, jovial. One had seemed so familiar, there was something about his voice—he had turned his head slowly, had immediately recognized the profile, his jacket straining over his portly stomach, that day he was supposed to meet Ilse, it had to be the same man. Hermann began to feel sweat droplets pearl at his hairline, his palms clammy; his hand slipped from the loop he grasped and for a moment he was left swaying unsteadily on his feet as he attempted to maintain his balance. The sweat trickled and his pulse began to thud, his muscles tense, his stomach churning; the person next to him jostled against him, the high-pitched squeal of the tram tracks drowned out the sounds around him, he had to get off, and fast. The tram stopped at Palace Park. He pushed his way through the bustling gaggle of passengers, his arms straight out in front of him as if he were slicing his way through the group, forcing his way to the doors. Once outside he took great gulps of air, in, out, he may no longer be on the tram but it was still there, perfectly stationary behind him at the stop. He started walking toward Solli Square without looking back. The tram rolled past him and he marched as fast as he could along Bygdøy allé with brisk steps—the lactic acid burned in his muscles as he rang Einar's doorbell, the same three short, sharp blasts he always gave to signal his arrival, the building door opened and it was only then, poised before the curved staircase, that his heart began to resume its normal rhythm once again, as if it had been in hibernation since the tram journey and had copious missed beats to catch up on.

Einar lets him into the apartment and peers at him as he takes off his jacket in the hallway.

"What is it?" Hermann asks him.

Einar takes a long drag of his cigarette, momentarily pausing with the smoke in his lungs before releasing it into the air.

"They've introduced the death penalty," he replies.

"What?"

"The death penalty."

The words hover in the air as if suspended between them as they stare at each other.

Einar takes a sip from his glass, smacking his lips as the brandy glides down his throat.

"What now?" Hermann asks him.

Einar takes another drag, blowing smoke rings into the air. His face is unexpectedly illuminated by a crooked smile.

"We carry on," he says. "We risk our lives, but damn it, we carry on regardless."

He shrugs his shoulders and makes his way down the hall toward the yellow room where they work.

Hermann has been to see Einar several times a week lately. They work in the yellow room, listening to news broadcasts from England at low volume on the wireless that Einar has managed to keep hidden in a box. They each note down what is said, the voice on the radio speaks quickly, and when the broadcast ends, Hermann sits down at the typewriter. They work all evening. On many occasions he has stayed all night. He has his own space in the red room, as long as there isn't anybody else there who needs it. Occasionally Einar has guests, that's what he calls them; I have guests, he says, nodding toward the red room. Einar's guests tend to stay for a few days, a week at most, and then they vanish. There are all kinds of people, young, old, men, women, sometimes a group and sometimes just one person. Einar has a lot of contacts, he's always ready to take a telephone call, arrange papers, help someone one step further in their journey. His only requirement is that his guests keep quiet, don't look out the windows, and never, under any circumstances, tell anyone that they stayed with him.

"So tell me, Hermann, have you spoken with the young Ilse Stern yet?" Einar asks when they've settled down to work in the yellow room. He always calls her that, "the young Ilse Stern." Hermann shakes his head.

"No," he replies, "I don't know what to say to her."

Einar laughs.

"Women trouble," he chuckles. "Possibly the only kind of trouble that I *don't* have to contend with."

"You should be glad about it too," Hermann tells him.

He exhales, groaning slightly.

"And what about at home?"

"Still skeptical about the art thing," Hermann says, rolling his eyes.

"Good," Einar says. "That's a good thing."

Ilse. The young Ilse Stern. Hermann hasn't managed to bring himself to speak to her yet. He has thought over and over again about what he might say. At times he's considered telling her everything: what had happened that day, exactly why he couldn't make it; he's imagined himself pleading with her to hear him out, purging himself of all of his secrets—at least then there would be one other person in the world who'd know what he was involved in. But he can't, he knows that, and he sits and mulls over all of his options. What would Ilse believe, what did she want to hear? It's been a long time now, days have turned into weeks and it might even be best just to allow the passing of time to continue, best to stay silent, cross his fingers, hope that she might forget.

They work late into the evening. Hermann's head throbs as he pulls on his jacket in the hallway. Einar opens the sliding door leading to the parlor, vanishing into the dark room and swiftly reappearing with a painting in his hands.

"Just some old nonsense I threw together," he says, handing it to Hermann, "but it might help you to have something to show for your efforts when you get home."

Hermann looks at it. A watercolor, a landscape in pinks and grays, and in the center of the picture is a bridge, fading into the distance, growing smaller and smaller as it extends into the background.

"So, we've been working on perspective, have we?" Hermann asks.

"That sounds about right," Einar chuckles, opening the front door.

It's cold and dark outside. Hermann walks quickly. He longs to be at home. Home. In his bed, sinking into nothingness beneath the sheets.

SONJA LEANS HER BACK AGAINST THE COLD cellar wall, squeezing her eyes closed again to adjust to the dimly lit room. All the building's residents are tightly packed in the space, a gathering of the underworld, poised and ready for the chance to clamber back up to ground level once again. There are only two lights, both situated in the middle of the room, lighting up the earthen floor, their feet, their faces lingering partly in darkness. They've been down here so many times now, it is almost as if they have their own reserved seats. In the farthest corner of the cellar they've created a little area with some benches. They carried down the ones that usually sit in the backyard in the summer, and there are bottles of water and other supplies in case they should find themselves confined there for an extended period of time.

They had done what they always do when the air raid siren sounds. They had picked up some extra clothes and a few blankets and had made their way down to the ground floor, opening the cellar door and scrambling down the steep staircase. She and Ilse had gone first, followed by their mother and then by their father, who carried Miriam in his arms. Several of their neighbors were already down there. Ole Rustad had lit the lamps. He's sitting next to Anna now, his large hand resting on her swollen belly. It can't be many weeks before the baby is due. Anna moans softly, reaching for the small of her back. Their two daughters, Karin and Lilly, sit by Miriam. All three draw pictures, utterly absorbed by what they're doing. Their mother had stored some colored pencils and paper in the cellar to help Miriam pass the time and to stop her from feeling afraid. The three girls are sitting on the bench pushed up against one wall, leaning on a chest that they use as a make-shift table.

There are eight apartments, two on each floor, and everyone from the building is assembled in the cellar. No, actually, not all of them. Dagny Larsen from the first floor isn't there, Sonja can see that now. Dagny danced and sang at the German Theater down on Stortingsgata. Once, back in spring, Sonja had seen a man in uniform enter the building; he had smiled and strided into the apartment on the first floor. Rumors spread to the floors above faster than the smell of fresh bread: Dagny Larsen had a German companion.

The cellar is silent tonight. Nobody utters a word, not even a whisper. Ilse sits hiding her face behind a book, making a show of reading the pages, while Hermann is seated on the bench opposite them, his shoulders hunched, his head resting in his hands. He looks up at Ilse. The new family from the fourth floor are huddled together in the far corner. Sonja hasn't said a word to them since they arrived, she hasn't greeted them at all. Whenever she has happened upon them they've looked the other way, hurrying in or out with brisk steps. According to Ingeborg they're on the other side. It was as if the whole building and its residents had undergone a change after the family had moved in; everything had grown quiet. In the past it had been quite nice in the cellar. Ole Rustad used to tell jokes, the ridiculous kind without any point or purpose, but everyone had laughed all the same. Now there's nothing to be heard, just silence. Seconds and minutes pass them by in the cold, damp space.

Her mother sits with a book in her lap, *The Forager's Guide to Free Foods in the Wild*; she looks as if she's carefully pondering the contents. They had tried planting in the backyard, digging up the dirt around the washing line poles to make space for something that might have become a little vegetable garden, but it was too shady; the sun barely managed to peek over the rooftops before disappearing once again behind the buildings that flanked their own; nothing to speak of had thrived in that little patch of earth. Her father sits by her mother's side, his eyes closed. Very suddenly they both look old. There's something about them, her mother's expression, the small wrinkles on her forehead, her father resting his head against the cellar wall. She can picture their expressions when she breaks the news about her plans; her father's eyes, dark, desperate, her mother's tearing up, maybe, or flashing with anger, the pitch of her voice increasing until it becomes a high screech, reproachful, filled with accusations, think of your father, for God's sake think of your poor father.

Sonja hasn't said anything, not yet. The right moment just hasn't come along, she hasn't figured out the right words to use, doesn't know how to start, how to lay everything out. But she does have news.

She had been nervous on the day that she went to the theater. She had neatly folded and wrapped her costume in brown paper. A secretary in a tight-fitting suit and small, round glasses had greeted her, smiling, and had asked Sonja to follow her to the sewing room. Mr. Østli was waiting there, she explained; he was in charge of hiring.

They ascended a carpeted staircase and entered the sewing room. Inside the room were rows and rows of sewing machines, boxes of bobbins, a whole wall of fabric rolls, and in one corner Sonja could see an actor being measured up as he hummed aloud to warm up his voice. The light beamed in through the oval windows, and a sweet aroma of perfume and theater makeup filled the air. A few of the seamstresses glanced in her direction as she entered. Helene stood behind a table and measured out a length of red velvet material, nodding encouragingly at Sonja as she passed.

Mr. Østli was sitting behind a desk. Without looking up he asked her to sit down, and the secretary quietly left the office. Sonja placed the package in her lap; her palms were sweating, she felt the brown paper soften beneath her clammy fingers, Mr. Østli seated opposite her, immersed in a stack of paper. He looked young, younger than she had imagined, his dark hair neatly combed and flat against his head, his face narrow, his nose straight. A half-smoked cigarette lay in an ashtray, a thick veil of smoke rising from within.

"I hear that you are looking for work," he said, his gaze still fixed on his papers. "What prompts you to choose the theater, may I ask?"

"It's my dream," Sonja said, her tone so assured that she surprised even herself; it suddenly seemed so simple, so obvious, self-evident. "I have my papers here."

She opened her purse, taking out her course qualification documents and placing them on the desk.

Mr. Østli glanced at them briefly before pushing them aside. Finally he looked up at her. He remained motionless, gazing at her.

"May I offer you a cigarette?" he asked, smiling and presenting a packet with a white cigarette poking out from within.

Sonja reached out, took it, Mr. Østli stood up, retrieved a lighter from his jacket pocket, leaned in toward her; she could feel his breath against her forehead as he lit her cigarette.

"May I ask how old you are, Sonja?"

"Almost nineteen," she replied, but as she uttered the words she felt the smoke clog her throat; she leaned forward and coughed, tears blurring her vision.

Mr. Østli laughed.

"I could tell at once that you weren't a smoker," he said. He took the cigarette from her, promptly stubbing it out. Leaning against the desk, he cocked his head to one side with a broad smile.

"We could use more seamstresses," he said. "But I can't take on anyone new before the first of December. At that point we'll begin making preparations for the upcoming performances."

He leaned toward her and took her hand, which still rested on the brown paper package, his own hand large, his palm dry.

"How would that suit you, Miss Sonja? You are a miss, aren't you?"

Sonja nodded.

"But what about the sample, don't you want to look at it?" Sonja asked, withdrawing her hand from his and starting to untie the twine that had held the parcel together.

"I've no doubt that you are an outstanding seamstress," Mr. Østli told her. "You can leave the sample costume here with me. The first of December, are we agreed?"

He held out his hand, nodding toward the package in brown paper.

"We can take care of the paperwork when you begin," he said, placing the parcel on a shelf behind his desk. "Now! I think you ought to go out and celebrate your new employment."

He strode over to his office door and opened it.

"You are a very pretty young woman, Sonja. I am most certain that you will brighten up our sewing room."

It had been nothing like what she had expected it to be; she had prepared answers to all manner of questions, readied herself to sit and brag about her achievements. Now her sample costume lay on a shelf; he might never open the package to look at it. For a long while she sat on a bench in the park outside the theater, empty, exhausted, joyful, afraid; feelings whirled around inside her, thudding, father, mother, the sewing room and its plethora of fabrics, the carpets, the oval windows, the shop—the words she'd have to utter at home.

Sonja can sense it, just how tired she is; her eyelids feel dry, her temples throb. There aren't many hours left before she'll have to be up and about again. She rests her head on her father's shoulder, takes in his smell, his presence, his distance. He places an arm around her, patting her gently, like a child, just like he's always done. She jumps when the signal sounds. They're out of danger. They can make their way back up to their apartment. Drowsily they climb the steep cellar stairs, up to the third floor and into the apartment, her mother and father to their divan in the living room and she, Ilse, and Miriam into their bedroom.

Sonja lies awake; she can hear Miriam and Ilse, soft sounds as they gently exhale in their sleep. The light is on in the living room, her father is sitting in the armchair. She ought to just get it over with now, go to him, confess everything, face the inevitable. He's sitting out there, she could just get up and out of her bed, it's no distance at all. Sonja turns over to face the wall, pulling the bedsheets tight around her and curling her legs up under her. The pattern on the wallpaper, the light that frames the open door into the living room, she can hear him flipping through the pages of a book, then placing it down on the floor, stretching. He puts out the light. Footsteps over to the divan. The darkness makes the apartment so quiet, tightly sealed.

IN THE AFTERNOON ILSE BUMPS INTO
Hermann in the passageway. Her mother's high-
pitched screeches are entrenched in her memory,
firmly embedded and pounding away, she just has to
get out, down to the bridge by the river.

But then there he is, Hermann Rød, larger than life
and standing before her very eyes. He's on his way in,
she's on her way out. The front gate clangs closed behind
him. He almost seems to jump at the sight of her,
plunging his hands inside his coat pockets, his shoulders suddenly hunched, avoiding eye contact. More
than anything Ilse wants to stride right past him, she's
not ready for this, not now, she feels jittery, on edge,
but she stops, her body seizes up, everything tenses.

He looks worn out, pale, tired, his face ashen. For a
brief second she almost feels a pang of sympathy.

"Ilse Stern," he says, just as he always does when he
sees her. He looks at her, smiling cautiously, apologeti-
cally, but it isn't *his* smile, it doesn't really seem to be
him standing before her.

"Hermann Rød," she replies, gazing right past him, long and hard.

They linger by the bins. A bitter draft rushes into the passageway, picking up the smell of the rubbish.

Ilse hasn't seen Hermann for twenty-one days. It has been exactly twenty-one days since he stood her up, and she has painstakingly counted each and every one of them. There has been only one exception to their separation: She felt his gaze pierce the darkness of the underground cellar on the night the air raid sirens had gone off, but she had taken cover behind her book, only very occasionally peering over the top, eyes flickering before looking down once again.

"Where are you going?" Hermann asks her.

"Out for a walk," she says, looking at the door.

"Is everything okay?"

"What?"

"Is everything okay, Ilse?"

"Everything is *great*, Hermann."

Ole Rustad appears from around the corner.

"Well well well, this is where the young people spend their time nowadays, is it?" he says, smiling at them both. "Dressed more appropriately for the weather today, I see," he says to Ilse. He doffs his cap at the pair and disappears through the front gate. It clangs loudly as it closes again. Silence descends once more.

She's gone over this in her head, this exact moment, all the many possible versions of the same event. She's imagined Hermann begging for her forgiveness, stroking her hair from her face, her own annoyance, delight, cool distance, warmth, understanding, she's covered every base. Apart from this one, that is, as she stands before him, unmoving, timid.

"Hey, Ilse?" Hermann's voice is soft; he fiddles with his key ring. "I'm so sorry." He's still not looking at her. The keys slip from his grasp and he bends over to pick them up, placing them in his pocket. She can hear him continuing to fidget with them.

"That I didn't come, I mean."

She says nothing, opening her mouth and closing it again; she can't allow everything that has been swirling around inside her head to pour out now.

"Did you wait for long?"

"No."

She answers almost before he has asked the question, shaking her head.

"I'm glad," he replies. "I don't know what to say. I had a good reason for not being there."

She nods. Silence. Ole Rustad drives past in his taxi, beeping his horn and waving at them. Hermann scratches his cheek with his slim fingers, she's always liked his hands; he raises his eyebrows, his eyes the same piercing blue.

"It won't be long before the snow starts," he says after a while. "Promise me that we'll take a ski trip together after the first snowfall, Ilse? Just you and me?"

He looks at her, properly now, directly in the eye as if everything were back to normal between them. She doesn't answer him, why doesn't she say anything, anything at all, but then there is something else, something she can't let him see, a tickle in her throat, something brimming over, reopening the wound, threatening to unravel. She walks past him, toward the gate, pushes it open and runs across Biermanns gate as she hears the resounding clang of the gate closing behind her.

The Akerselva River rushes past the bridge. It's been raining for days now. She leans against the railing, watching the way the torrent cascades over the stones, working its way down and away. Everything starts this autumn, she suddenly thinks. So stupid. Does anything ever start with autumn, really? Autumn brings darkness, quiet, rest, death, trees lose their leaves and the earth grows hard. In a week it will be November. She draws the fresh air deep into her lungs, tastes it, bitter and tinged with something, a scent, a rupture, winter. Maybe the snow will come soon. She feels herself smile. And maybe, just maybe, things are different from what she had thought. Maybe everything starts with the first snow.

ISAK HAD BEEN AWAKE FOR ONLY A FEW moments before he heard the knock at the door. As was his habit every morning, he had been sitting on the edge of the bed and thinking about the day ahead of him. His sense of fatigue was more pronounced than usual this morning. The air raid siren had blared throughout the city the previous night, and he can't have caught all that many hours of sleep. He had been thinking about the order he needed to complete that day, due for collection at noon.

Hanna sits up in bed with an abrupt lurch. She turns to face him, her hair disheveled. Her nightdress slips to reveal a bony shoulder protruding from the garment's neckline.

"There was a knock at the door, Isak."

He hears Miriam in the bedroom stirring in her bed, mumbling to herself. Another knock. Isak lights the lamps, slips his feet into his slippers, and shuffles toward the front door.

He turns the latch and opens the door just wide enough that he can peer through the gap.

"Isak Stern?"

Two men are standing outside. One is large and muscular, wearing a light-colored coat, while the other is tall and slim with round spectacles; the lenses have steamed up, and in his hands he holds a sheaf of papers, the cold air of the stairwell seeping into the apartment.

"Yes," Isak replies.

"We have an order for your arrest."

He hears Hanna's footsteps as she crosses the room. She enters the hallway where he stands. She has pulled her dressing gown on over her nightdress, tightly knotting it around her waist as she glances from side to side.

"What's going on?"

The men push their way into the narrow hallway, closing the door behind them. The man wearing the spectacles passes a sheet of paper to Isak before taking a handkerchief from his coat pocket and removing his glasses to polish the lenses.

All males over the age of fifteen years in possession of identification cards stamped with the letter J are to be arrested, with no upper age limit. Arrestees will be transported to Kirkeveien 23, Oslo.

Hanna remains close, leaning in to read the document in Isak's hands.

"But he hasn't done anything wrong."

Nobody responds.

Arrests will be carried out on Monday 26 October at 06:00. The document is a mass of words, they blend and flow and blur into one another; crooked symbols, letters, commas, and periods, line after line after line. His eyes flicker over the page, he reads the top section, the bottom section, he understands and yet still he fails to, Monday, it's Monday — the paper is stiff, he holds it in both hands, too many words all at once, he hasn't properly woken yet, and he's hungry. Terribly, terribly hungry.

"Bring clothing, your ration card, and all of your identification documents." The other man speaks now, the man in the light-colored coat; he points at the sheet of paper where everything he has just said is written down.

"But when will he be allowed to come home again?" Hanna asks. "I don't understand."

"Mrs. Stern," he continues, "you are under strict instructions to report daily to the police station."

Your financial assets are to be seized. Your bank account will be closed and your safety deposit boxes emptied. He has to tell Hanna, he has to catch her alone. The cigar tin. The money would last them a while. At least until he's back with them; until then they can live on what he had hidden in the chest of drawers.

The girls have wandered into the living room. Wide-eyed and standing in nothing but their nightdresses, Sonja lifts Miriam into her arms and holds her close.

He was too late. It is the only thought that runs through his head. Too late. If only he had made a decision, if only he had known just how little time he had at his disposal, he would have done what was needed. They could have crossed the border to neutral Sweden by now, if only he had followed through on his plans. He even had a name; for days he had contemplated contacting a man by the name of E. Vindju in Frogner. But he hadn't, and now it was too late, they had gotten to him first.

He turns to face them, his girls, their feet bare on the cold floor.

"You need to pack your things now," said the man in the light-colored coat.

It is cold outside. Isak turns and looks up at the windows on the third floor. They stand at the living room window, four dark shapes, watching him. He had pulled each of them close before leaving, one after the other, had held on to Hanna, buried his face into her dark hair, brought his lips to her ear and then, so quietly that nobody else could hear, he had whispered just three words. He could have said so much more. I'll be back.

Look after yourselves. God bless you. He didn't say any of those things, he wasn't thinking about those things. The cigar tin. The cigar tin in the drawer. He spoke as softly as he could.

They walk toward Vogts gate. He can hear the shrill screeching of the tram as it trundles by, footsteps on asphalt, his shallow breathing, his rumbling stomach. The cold air smarts within his chest; soon there will be snow, he has never much liked the snow.

EVERYTHING IS SO QUIET IN THE DAYS that follow. The slightest of sounds creates an echo. A cup against the kitchen sink. The creak of a cupboard door. Colored pencils against a piece of paper.

They navigate their way around one another, hushed, cautious; there's a gaping hole in the apartment, it expands to fill the rooms, makes it difficult to breathe.

Ilse stands in the doorway between the hallway and the living room, rooted to the spot and staring into the room. She can see her father's gray wool slippers beneath the divan, one resting slightly on top of the other. Mum hasn't tidied up today, either, she hasn't folded the divan back in its place and the duvet is still curled at the end of the mattress, the sheets wrinkled, strands of her mother's dark hair visible on the white pillowcase.

Her mother sits in the armchair by the window. Her eyes are closed; perhaps she's sleeping again. Miriam lies beneath the table, drawing. She's almost stopped speaking altogether, only gives yes or no answers, she's preoccupied, doesn't listen properly to anything that anyone says to her. Sonja washes up in the kitchen.

The sunlight cuts through the living room windows at an angle. Her mother's face is bathed in light. Her hair is pinned up yet untidy, her skin taut over her cheekbones, a shell that could crack and break at a moment's notice. She turns around, away from the dazzling sunlight, rests her head against the back of the chair.

They hadn't moved an inch for a good long while after their father disappeared that day. They had all just stood there, as if waiting for him to reappear on the street any minute, to wave up at them, shrug his shoulders to let them know it had all been a gross misunderstanding, that they had the wrong man.

Their mother was the first to move. She crossed the room, tearing each drawer from the dresser and pulling out item after item. Her hands moved quickly. The pile on the floor grew and grew, underwear, shirts, balls of yarn and unfinished needlework, knitting needles, scraps of fabric, their father's undershirts. Then she stood up. She was holding a cigar tin in her hands.

"What is it, Mum?" Sonja asked.

Their mother carried the tin over to the table and removed the lid.

"Isak," she whispered softly, "Isak, what have you done?"

Sonja took care of the money, sorting it into small piles, carefully counting it every night. It was all they had to live on, and they had no idea for how long that would be the case.

Their mother reported to the police station every day. She left the apartment after breakfast and would be gone for several hours before returning home, washed out and withdrawn. Often she would go to sleep as soon as she came back, either on the divan or sitting in the armchair by the window. She didn't care much for making meals, couldn't face keeping the house in order. Her hair became lank and flat; she no longer set it in rollers, instead simply pinning it up with a few clasps. One day she had worn her skirt back to front, and when Ilse had pointed it out, her mother had looked at her, her gaze vacant, then opened the door and left.

She didn't sleep at night. Ilse could hear her tossing and turning, whispering to herself. One night Ilse had awoken to find her mother standing in the bedroom. She had been breathing heavily, her eyes darting around the room as if she suddenly didn't recognize her surroundings.

"Why are you standing there?" Ilse murmured, sitting up in her bed.

Her mother said nothing. In her white nightdress she looked almost transparent.

"Mum?"

"Are you talking to me? Don't talk to me, Sonja."

"It's Ilse, Mum. You need to go back to bed."

Her mother didn't move.

"Can you come with me?" she whispered after a moment.

Ilse had followed her into the living room, tucking the eiderdown in around her. Her mother had stared into the dark room, her body slender and delicate, her face all that was visible where the eiderdown ended; helpless and heavy with anxiety, she had looked so small.

At the police station, their mother had met other Jewish women in the same position. They weren't regulars at the synagogue, but the community was small and their mother knew many of them. All of the men had been taken, all on that same morning, and none of the women knew where they had gone, though there were rumors that they had been sent to a work camp in northern Norway.

On Friday, their mother hadn't emerged from her bed again after returning home from the police station; she had simply refused. Ilse and Sonja had set the table just like their mother used to every Friday afternoon. The white tablecloth was stiff, the candles ready. Their mother lay facing the wall, utterly silent.

"Don't you want to light the candles, Mum? Everything's ready. Don't you want to bless the candles?"

Their mother gave no response. Sonja crouched down by the divan, stroking her back, trying to encourage her to get up. She bristled at Sonja's touch, pinched tight like a set of forceps where she lay, her arms wrapped around her legs. They had eaten their dinner that Friday, Ilse, Sonja, and Miriam, the white candles on the table beside them, unlit. Ilse couldn't remember that ever happening before.

Miriam shifts position beneath the table, her head poking out from one side.

"Do you know what I'm going to be when I grow up, Ilse?" she whispers. "I'm going to be a flower lady."

"Oh really? And what does a flower lady do?"

"Well, they stand in shops. And they sell bunches of flowers."

She holds out a drawing: a girl in a red dress, flowers in her hands, and at the top of the sheet of paper is a yellow orb, Miriam's trademark, a large, golden sun sending long beams in all directions.

"The sun is always shining in your pictures, Miriam."

"Yes, because it's easy to draw. It's just a yellow circle with lines coming out of it."

She disappears back under the table.

Ilse hasn't seen any more of Hermann. It's been two weeks since her father disappeared; she hasn't been able to talk to him about it yet. Every time she took out the rubbish she'd hoped that she might bump into him. She'd linger there much longer than necessary, fumbling by the rubbish bins, enveloped by the brisk, bitter, cold air pocket of the passageway. Why didn't he ever come?

It was chilly outside; it would be snowing any day now. Then they'd go skiing. He'd said so himself. For a moment the thought gives her a tiny thrill. She walks into the kitchen, crosses the room to the window, carefully opens it, and sticks a hand out into the open air. It *is* cold. It's just a case of waiting. Waiting for her father. Waiting for the snow. Just waiting.

S ONJA UNHOOKS HER WINTER COAT FROM
the peg in the hallway, laces her boots, pulls
on her red hat, and pokes her head into the living room.

"I'll be off, then," she says.

Ilse sits in her father's armchair with Miriam on her lap. The two of them are reading fairy tales together. Their mother has gone to bed. Again. Sonja can just make out the contour of her curved spine beneath the crumpled eiderdown.

"I won't be long. A few hours, maybe."

Ilse smiles at her, nods.

"Say hi from me," she says.

A bracing November gust rounds the corner of the building, a thin veil of frost over the grass in the backyard.

Sonja crosses Vogts gate and walks toward the river, on her way to St. Hanshaugen to visit a friend. Well, perhaps visit isn't quite the right word; it isn't exactly as if anybody is expecting her, there is no table set ready for her arrival.

A week ago she and Ilse had bumped into Marie, an old classmate. Marie was from a Jewish family and told a familiar story: The police had come to their home on that Monday morning and had taken her father and two brothers. Now it was just Marie and her mother left, the pair of them alone in an apartment on Bjerregaards gate. Pop by one day, she'd told Sonja. At first Sonja had thought it was just something Marie had said to be polite, but then she'd started to think about it some more. Maybe they knew something, Sonja thought, maybe they'd heard from their own loved ones.

On the day their father had been taken, Ilse and Sonja had taken the tram into the city center. Their mother had found a blanket, a pair of boots, and a wool sweater and had packed them inside a brown paper bag; they should take it to Kirkeveien 23, she said, see if they could see their father. The tram was full, it was an ordinary Monday in Oslo, people were going about their ordinary lives, talking, laughing, and then there they were, Sonja and Ilse, perched at the back of the carriage with the paper bag between them.

There were guards stationed outside Kirkeveien 23.

"What do we do now?" Sonja asked.

"We'll tell them we want to speak to Isak Stern," Ilse said. "Let's just go over."

Ilse approached one of the guards, a young man, explaining why they were there. There was something about her tone, she sounded almost angry, a headstrong child who wouldn't take no for an answer.

"There's nobody here anymore," the guard said. "They've been gone for a while now."

"But, I mean, where are they?" Ilse asked. "We wanted to deliver this."

She pointed at the paper bag. The guard glanced around him.

"I don't know where they're going," he told her after a moment's pause. "There were trucks and buses; they arrived and drove them away."

An older guard walked in their direction.

"You can't be here," he shouted. "Go on! Get lost!"

Kirkeveien 23, that was the last they knew of their father's whereabouts. Now Sonja has started to wonder if Marie knows something else. What had happened to the men afterward; where had they been taken? Had Marie's father and brothers sent word somehow?

It feels as if it has been forever since she was out on her own, forever since she had any time to herself. The past few weeks had been filled with so many practical tasks.

It's odd, she thinks: Their father was arrested, the shop was closed down, their mother was losing all sense of reason, and what was it that occupied her own thoughts? The daily routine, that's what, the work that allowed them to leave behind one day and move on to the next. Ilse helped out too, but she didn't carry any real responsibility, she had more freedom, she was more of an assistant than anything, she lent a hand from time to time and then went her own way with a good conscience. Sonja never went anywhere, she always stayed at home with their mother, with Miriam; maybe she ought to get out more often, just to find some space to breathe. They reacted so differently to things, she and Ilse. Ilse would fly into a temper, raising her voice and stomping around, but Sonja clammed up, hardly saying a word, blunt. Instead she entered the kitchen, did the washing up, worked like a machine that couldn't be deactivated. She still hadn't said anything to her mother, or to Ilse for that matter. Everything was so different at home since her father's disappearance—how could she possibly bring up the theater? She had tried talking to her mother once when she had been lying on the divan. Ilse was out and Miriam was in the bedroom with Karin.

"Mum?" Sonja sat on the edge of the bed. "Mum, there's something I need to tell you."

Her mother lay motionless. Sonja leaned over her to

check if her eyes were closed. They weren't, and she lay staring at the wall in front of her, the index finger of her left hand gently stroking the wallpaper, as if she were trying to rub away a stain.

"I've . . ."

She made it no further. Her mother turned around abruptly and stared at her.

"Can you take Karin back up to the Rustads'?" she whispered. "They're making such a racket out there. I can't bear having other people's children around."

She turned away again, wrapped the eiderdown tightly around her, and closed her eyes. Disappeared.

Sonja hovered at the doorway, peering into the bedroom. Miriam and Karin lay on the floor, each drawing something, not speaking a word to each other, no sound to be heard but that of pencils on paper.

She left her mother in peace. It wouldn't do to blurt out news like this, not now. Anyway, she wasn't due to start for another three weeks; she'd find another opportunity, sneak it into conversation somewhere. Plus, it could be good news now that the shop had been closed down and they had no money coming in. But to say so, to allow the words to cross her lips, that would be difficult, impossible.

Something else had come up too, just before their father had disappeared. One day Sonja was locking up the shop for the day only to find Helene standing right outside.

"I hadn't thought about the fact that you're a Jew," Helene said. "Are you a proper Jew, or just a little bit Jewish?"

Sonja looked at her. What was she trying to say?

They took a walk through the cemetery at Gamle Aker. Helene had heard some of the seamstresses commenting on Sonja's surname. Stern, one of them had said, isn't that Jewish? Would the theater director really employ a Jewish seamstress? He was appointed by the government, after all.

"Don't tell anyone," Helene advised her. "Wait until they see how good you are, then maybe it won't be so bad."

"But the theater director," said Sonja. "Does he know I'm Jewish?"

"I don't know about that," Helene continued. "But he's not one of the bad ones, I don't think. Lots of people like him, even if he *is* one of them."

She makes her way up Bjerregaards gate, reading the small plaques bearing the numbers of each of the apartment buildings. There's a tailor shop on the corner, a sign hanging in the large windows at street level: *Fish skin shoes.*

On one of the first days after her father's disappearance, she and Ilse had gone to their shop. It had been a sunny day, and a faint, dwindling light had glimmered on the shop windows.

It was only then that they had seen it, something on one window, a word, just one little word scrawled in white, cursive script: *Jew.*

"Was that why he was always washing the windows?" Ilse had whispered.

They had tried the front door. It was locked. They had no idea where the key had gone after they had delivered it to the police. A note had been affixed to the front door: *Closed until further notice.*

She stops outside number eleven. Makes her way through the gate that leads to a narrow backyard.

Nobody opens when she knocks at the door to Marie's apartment. Sonja waits there for a little while, knocking one more time. The door of the opposite apartment opens and an elderly woman sticks her head out.

"Are you looking for the Abrahamsens?" she asks.

Sonja nods.

"Well, they're not home. Mrs. Abrahamsen and her daughter left early one morning, can't have been more than a week ago," she continues.

"Where did they go?" Sonja asks.

"Well, *I* certainly don't know. Are you a relative?"

"I'm a friend of Marie," Sonja replies.

The old lady closes the door behind her and approaches Sonja.

"I don't know this for certain," she whispers, "but I don't imagine they'll be back."

Sonja looks at her. "What do you mean?"

"The Abrahamsens had a cat. On the morning that they left, they knocked at my door and asked me very nicely if I would take her." She hesitates before continuing. "I think they've crossed the border."

"Crossed the border?

"Crossed the border and fled to Sweden. They didn't say where they were going, but they were wrapped up well and seemed a little jumpy. I haven't seen them since."

She gives Sonja a kind smile before returning to her apartment, closing the door behind her.

Sonja takes a different route home. She walks up Ullevålsveien, cuts across the road diagonally, and carries on toward St. Hanshaugen, right to the top of the hill, standing there for a moment and looking out over the city. The clouds linger heavily in the sky; she can see a vessel just off Nesoddlandet, a gray block sailing outward across the fjord. It would be so wonderful to travel, she thinks, wonderful and terrifying, she can't really decide which. What should she say when she gets back in, should she tell the others that Marie and her mother have fled to Sweden, what would they make of it all, would they start considering doing the same thing? And what about their father? They had no way to warn him. And the theater, the job that awaited her, was she really prepared to leave all that behind too? Perhaps they'd have to. Perhaps when the theater director found out who he'd employed he'd tell her that a Jew couldn't be permitted to work at present, not in his theater at any rate.

Sonja decides to tell the others that Marie and her mother weren't at home when she called. It is the truth, after all. She will mull over the Sweden thing herself, maybe mention it to Ilse. They can take some time to consider it, look into it again in a little while.

Tiny, cold drops start to fall from the sky and she runs fast, the gravel crunching beneath her feet.

THE SMELL HITS HERMANN THE MOMENT he enters the passageway. Rotten, like food that has been left out for too long, a dead animal. He stops by the rubbish bins, lifts the lid, and sniffs; no, it's not coming from in there. Maybe it's coming from the backyard, a rat, he's seen them enough times, stiff wretches with vacant, glassy stares. The grass is almost white, it rustles beneath his feet. He glances up at Ilse's window, sees only darkness. He feels a sense of trepidation.

Lately he's spent every afternoon with Einar, every evening too, for that matter. They've worked all night to get the secret newspaper out. He's managed to catch a few hours' sleep in the red room before he's had to get up again to make it to work at the brewery. Half-conscious he's worked, sleeping during his breaks, sitting with his head resting against the wall. Everything around him seems dizzying, the sounds so loud, threatening, the clinking of the glass bottles, heavy crates crashing to the ground; he jumps at the slightest thing. He can't go on like this. The foreman is out to get him, always asking uncomfortable questions. At home his mother and father are at it too, complaining about the debauched life they're convinced that he's leading, nights spent in drunken depravity, reminders about the work that he's neglecting. He's tired of taking it all without being able to defend himself, tired of the foolish paintings he has to show off when he gets home, landscapes and perspective pieces; he's on thin ice.

He hasn't been to see Ilse. He should have, really. Should have ventured the few steps across the stairwell, knocked at her door, helped out, been there; after all that had happened, he really should have done the right thing. But he's kept his distance, and for what? He's shut himself up with Einar for company, lain in the red room, the safe yet unsafe red room; he's closed his eyes and tossed and turned, in and out of his slumber, sweating, cold. But he's thought of her. He's thought of her often.

One evening over in Frogner they had each been sitting in their chair in the lounge when Einar had brought out a bottle of brandy, pouring a generous measure into two large glasses.

"Cheers," said Einar. "Here's to . . . something or other."

He raised his glass. Hermann didn't say a word. He felt the throbbing pain, the warmth, the soothing heat of the brandy as it slid down his throat. He glanced at the bottle—half-full—he could ask for another, head to bed dizzy, maybe even catch a whole night's sleep, peaceful, numb.

"And the young Miss Ilse Stern," Einar said, a serious expression on his face. "Have you managed to speak to her?"

Another sip. Warm. Warm and cold all at once, a shiver down his spine; he would have loved to have said yes, that he *had* spoken to her, that they were ready, that all there was left to do was to set things in motion. He wished he were more efficient, that he spoke with clarity and conviction, but the walls here, the walls at home, the air outside, he couldn't breathe, there was something there, pressing in on him all the time, his thoughts were hazy, like tangled ropes; he doesn't know where to begin to unravel it all, to find the end, and regardless of how he pulls, things only ever seem to become more inextricably entwined. Hermann shook his head.

He had told Einar about Isak, about the shop that had been closed down, about those who had been left behind. Should they do something, get away? He was so concerned about them, so concerned that something might happen to them. Should he bring them here, to the red room? Could Einar organize something, get things moving? And what about him, what should he do, should he do anything at all?

"How many of them?" Einar had asked.

"Ilse and her sisters, Sonja and Miriam, and their mother too. Miriam's only five."

"Do they have any family in the city?"

"Not anymore. Their grandmother died last year. There's no one else."

"It's the men who are most vulnerable, but you never know. I think you should talk to Ilse."

But he hasn't. Not yet. Perhaps he's cowardly. Selfish, maybe. He had bumped into Ilse in the passageway a week ago, she had been standing there with a bag of rubbish in one hand, fiddling with the lid of the bin. He had asked if she had wanted to take a walk and she had nodded.

They had strolled down through Grünerløkka, through Birkelunden Park, along Thorvald Meyers gate. He could hear Einar's voice in the back of his mind; now, he thought, now, you have to do it now. He cleared his throat, closed his mouth, opened it, cleared his throat once more, but there were no words, he couldn't work out how to begin, what should his first word be, the very first to cross his lips?

Ilse walked by his side; it was silent but for the

sound of their footsteps and his ridiculous spluttering. When they reached Olaf Ryes Square they sat down on a bench. Some children played tag, a woman begged. He laid his arm across the back of the bench, she looked at him, and suddenly, as if in one soft, swift, effortless shift, she moved in close and pressed her face into his coat. He could hear her crying. He remained there, holding her close to him, moving his lips to her white hat, breathing in the scent of her. Should he really tell her now; concerns, questions, thoughts that would niggle at her, open the wound, was it the right thing to do?

"Ilse Stern," he said, stroking her head. "Kind, beautiful Ilse."

She lifted her head and gazed up at him. Her eyes were puffy, her skin dry, snot running from her nose.

"Beautiful?" she said, her voice thick.

"Yes, beautiful," he said. "Beautiful Ilse Stern."

She smiled at him, wiping her nose with the sleeve of her jacket.

"Do you know something, Hermann?" she said after a moment's silence. "I waited a long time for you that day."

"Really?" he said, smiling. "How long?"

"A long time. A very long time, actually."

No, he hadn't said anything, they had simply sat there together for a good long while, talking, looking at each other. Ilse had perked up, and it was so good to see her happy again. He couldn't just blurt out everything that he had on his mind without warning, you might all have to leave behind everything that you have, no, he didn't want to ruin the mood. Maybe it was selfish, maybe it was cowardly, but he hadn't said a word.

Now he's standing outside her door. He lifts a hand and knocks three, four times. From within the apartment he hears a shuffling on the other side of the door. It opens and Mrs. Stern cautiously peers out at him. Hermann hasn't seen her since Isak was arrested, and what he sees in that moment shocks him. Her blouse is stained, not properly buttoned up, and she's wearing only an underskirt and a pair of large gray wool socks.

"The girls are out," she says, her voice weak, then closes the door before he can say anything else.

He stands where he is for a moment and wonders if he should knock again, ask when they might be back, if there's anything he can do for her. He hears her shuffling farther and farther away from the door and decides not to bother her anymore; maybe she needs some time on her own.

Ole Rustad walks up the stairs, smiling.

"It'll be snowing before long," he declares gleefully, vanishing from sight as he bounds up the stairs two at a time.

People are making such a fuss about this impending snow, Hermann thinks; why does everyone keep rattling on about it? As if the snow could change anything, make anything simpler, conceal anything at all. But then he pauses and remembers that he and Ilse agreed to go skiing when the snow begins to fall. She hasn't said yes, but he is sure he can persuade her. Maybe he could talk to her then? It would be a good opportunity, far away from the city, far away from everything, the two of them out in the snow, Ilse Stern and Hermann Rød. Them and only them.

ENOUGH NOW. ILSE CAN FEEL IT IN HER stomach, radiating upward. Her mother, the cramped apartment, the mess, the dust, all the things that fill every corner, in drawers and cupboards, everything here and everything not here, everything that pours out, traps her, eats away at her, gnawing, stinging, like insects. Her mother is up and about, standing in the middle of the living room in her nightdress; it's the middle of the day, a Wednesday, her stockings have rolled down and gathered around her ankles, her veins snake up and around her arms, a greenish hue about them beneath her yellow skin. What had her mother just said? What had she just screeched? Her voice is loud and piercing, her expression drained. What had Ilse screamed back?

They stand glaring at each other. The whole room shakes. The words cling to the walls around them, wallowing on the floors beneath their feet, beneath the chairs, in the light that shines through the window.

They've been said out loud, there is no escaping them. Ilse opens her mouth.

"Out!"

Her mother points at the door, her arm outstretched, her eyes flashing black, blurred, her lips pursed. Sonja and Miriam are in the kitchen, neither moves a muscle; Ilse can hear them, breathing, a creak from a kitchen chair. Ilse grabs her brown coat from the peg and throws it over her shoulders, can't be bothered to button it up, she can do it outside. She reaches out for the white woolly hat on the shelf beside the others, steps into her dark brown lace-ups, hears her mother in the living room. She's crying. Wailing. But it was her mother who had asked her to leave, it was her mother who had screamed at her.

Ilse opens the door in one swift movement and as it slams closed behind her, she once again becomes aware of a strange feeling in the pit of her stomach, a sense of unease, as if her internal organs had all switched places, large intestine, small intestine, kidneys, bladder, everything displaced.

Ole Rustad is standing in the stairwell, leaning against the railing. Has he been standing there, listening in, spying on her? She gives him a small nod as she dashes down the stairs. He doesn't have the chance to say a word; she can't face his jokes, not today, his banal humor. He just stands there, like an extension of the railing, mute.

It'll be so good to get outside, get some fresh air. She doesn't know where she'll go, but right now anywhere is better than the claustrophobic, cramped little apartment where everything is such a tangled mess. She won't go back until evening, she'll just walk and walk through the whole city, her mother can sit there and fret for all she cares.

Just as she opens the door to step outside she sees that the snow has started to fall, a fine layer now covering the backyard. The pervasive rotten stench that had lingered earlier that day has gone. Now it smells, well, what is that smell, actually? Ilse inhales deeply. It smells like snow, she thinks.

She jumps when she catches sight of Hermann standing in the passageway. He's leaning against a wall with his back to her as she rushes around the corner. He turns around. He's wearing his blue anorak, the same that he'd been wearing when she'd seen him last, and a light gray hat pulled down low over his ears. He gives her a vacant stare, a smile forming on his lips, but his eyes don't follow suit, they look tired and weary; what's happening with Hermann?

"Back from work already?" she asks.

It can't be much past eleven o'clock. He says nothing in response, instead scratching his cheek, trying to come up with a new topic of conversation.

"Did you notice that it's started snowing?" he asks her. He's smiling now, a real, proper smile.

She nods.

"What do you say to taking a little ski trip, Ilse Stern?"

She faces him, silent. What is this all about? Does he really mean now, today? Why isn't he at work? Why is he standing there, raising his eyebrows at her? There's hardly any snow to speak of.

"There's barely any snow on the ground," she says, aware that she has to start somewhere.

"What about Maridalen, then," Hermann continues. "We can take the tram up to Kjelsås and head out from there."

This was definitely odd. Tempting, though, she couldn't deny it. She and Hermann in Maridalen, she's imagined it, in fact she's basically planned the whole thing, and it's only now that she begins to realize it. She ought to have been sitting and waiting for him, she ought to have been ready, lipstick applied in preparation; it shouldn't be happening like this. Nothing should happen like this.

"Well, I'm not exactly dressed for it," she says, shrugging in a slightly resigned manner.

"Can't you just go up and change?" Hermann suggests.

Ilse shakes her head. Up to her mother, her wailing and her nightdress and her demands and her complaints? Definitely not.

"But your skis are stored in the cellar, aren't they?"

They are, of course. Her pitch-seam boots too. She and Sonja shared a pair of skis and boots. Their father hadn't had the money to buy several pairs, so she and Sonja couldn't ever go out skiing together, but if she knew one thing it was that taking a ski trip would be the last thing on Sonja's mind today.

Hermann makes it sound so simple. Maybe it is simple, after all? Maybe it's just a case of going downstairs, picking up her skis and boots, and hopping on the tram? Getting away from everything. Maybe this is the best suggestion she's ever heard? A Wednesday morning. Ski and snow and fresh, crisp air. The thought brings a smile to her face. Even so, something isn't quite right about the whole situation.

"Hermann, why aren't you at work?"

He hesitates. But then he opens his mouth and answers her. He sounds cold and matter-of-fact, as if he were reciting his own address.

"They fired me."

S NOW. FINALLY. THERE IS SO MUCH SPACE out here. White and quiet, far from the city, just the two of them, Ilse Stern and Hermann Rød. It is just as he had imagined it. Ilse has been so quiet lately, and he's been quiet too, reflective; he has to say something soon, has to say the words out loud, there is so much he's been meaning to talk to her about. Like the fact that she might have to leave, cross the border, she and the rest of the family, that they might not have long to think things over. He has to be quick and straightforward, he can't drag it out, he can't frighten her; he just has to go over things slowly and calmly. But now that the time has come he can't quite remember how he'd planned to broach the subject, the words he'd decided to use; suddenly everything feels like a jigsaw puzzle and he's sitting with a thousand pieces in his lap and no idea where to place any of them. He can't even find a corner piece.

—

Ilse takes a fish cake and chews it slowly as he watches her, the movement of her temples; he can't face a single bite of his own.

"There's something I need to talk to you about," he begins, gently.

She looks at him. He has to keep going now, he has to explain everything, everything that's been going through his mind.

"Well, you know I've been spending a lot of time over in Frogner," he says, without knowing quite why he has chosen to begin in such a way.

"Is that why, do you think?" She takes another bite. "They must have given you a reason. Can't your father do anything?"

"What?"

"Can't your father help you?"

It's a mess, the pieces, they're all mixed up yet again. He doesn't answer; what can he possibly say? She holds his gaze.

"My father doesn't know about it," Hermann says after a slight pause. "Not yet. Anyway, there's not much he can do. It's the foreman's decision."

"But did he tell you why?"

He shakes his head.

"It must be because of your art, then. Don't you think, Hermann? That it might be the art thing?" She munches on her fish cake, her eyes wide and inquisitive as they look up at him from beneath her wool hat.

Art. He can't call it that, not really. He can't say it because it's not true. He's so tired of lying, making excuses, standing with a painting in hand as he waffles about perspective and color selection, things he hasn't the first idea about. Soon the entire room will be filled with watercolors. An abundance of alibis, evidence to offer up to his disinterested parents. Einar has even ensured that the paintings demonstrate a certain sense of progression, painting badly on purpose as he laughs at himself and the meaningless landscapes he creates. And Hermann stores the paintings behind the sofa in the living room, enthusiastically sharing everything he's been learning about over on Frederik Stangs gate. But no. That's exactly what he *never* does. He tells them nothing. He lies. He hasn't said a word about the yellow room, about how well-isolated it is with its blacked-out window. He hasn't said a word about the typewriter, or the wireless that Einar hides in a box, or the way they sit with their necks craned forward over the machinery, or just how quickly his fingers fly over the keys. He hasn't said a word about the distributors, the codes, the agreements that are never written down, the leaflets that change hands; circulating, filled with text, with news, printed on poor-quality paper. He hasn't said a word about his nerves, the feeling that pounds through his body, the alcohol that he consumes in worrying quantities, the prickling sensation in his hands, the dreams that follow him into sleep. He can't say a thing. They've introduced the death penalty. The police have already been to the door once. The newspaper could be discovered any day now.

That Saturday that he was supposed to meet Ilse at Olaf Ryes Square. The thing he can't tell her about. He and Einar had worked until quarter past four. He had put on his jacket and was ready to leave when he heard a sudden knock at the door, urgent, insistent, a voice in the stairwell.

"This is the police."

They had stood where they were, both motionless. Einar had looked at the floor and Hermann's fingers had clutched at the tickets in his pocket. Two voices in hushed conversation: We should wait, he has to come back sooner or later. Then more knocking, the sound of a match being lit, the smell of tobacco.

Hermann and Einar made their way deeper into the apartment, creeping along the long hallway and into the red room before closing the door softly behind them.

"How long will we have to wait here, do you think?" Hermann whispered.

Einar shook his head.

"They'll have to give up eventually."

Quarter to five, he would never make it; if only he had left a little earlier, he thought to himself, looking over at Einar, his forehead wrinkled.

They stood in the pitch-dark red room and peered out through a gap in the curtains. It had started to rain outside. It drummed against the asphalt.

It was just past nine when they saw two figures exit the front door of the building. He had spotted one of them again, that day he had been on the tram.

He can't say it's because of the art. He can't say anything. He just looks at her, smiling without moving his lips. He knows he has to talk to her, but no words come to him. Nothing. He only knows that he feels like getting up and walking, walking and walking and walking, far out into the snowy landscape, leaving everything behind. He's gone over it so many times in his head. He can breathe out here, and there's no pain, everything is so far away, the city, the yellow room, Einar, Biermanns gate; out here he can breathe. He places his hand on his knee, it edges toward Ilse's, he strokes his little finger against her thumb. It's afternoon, the sky is white with snow, and soon it will be dark. They can't get stuck out here, they need to turn around. He doesn't have a watch, doesn't quite know exactly where they are either, and their tracks have all but disappeared now, covered up by the heavy snow that's falling around them. All he wants to do is escape, never to return to the city. Just leave. Disappear into the snow. He turns and faces Ilse.

THAT NIGHT, SONJA DREAMS OF A BATHtub. All of a sudden it's there, at the side of a road, a large white tub at a slight angle on the sloping ground. There's a girl inside, she could be thirteen; the murky water makes the contours of her body difficult to distinguish. Her hair ripples like jellyfish tentacles. Her eyes are closed, her skin transparent, her hands and feet swollen as if they belong to the body of someone much older, her nails long and yellowed, like pieces of apple peel. Sonja reaches a hand into the water; it's cold, like burying her hand in snow. The girl in the bathtub opens her eyes, just slightly, revealing a dark cleft as her eyelids slowly open; her eyes are black, her lips move, forming something close to a smile, or is it a call for help? She says something but it's impossible to hear, only the sound of gurgling can be made out. And it rains, large droplets, everything is wet, the water streaming down the road. The water in the bathtub is still, the rain doesn't touch the surface, but there are noises reverberating from within, words,

louder now, clearer, everything is disappearing, everything is disappearing.

She wakes up at the kitchen table, her head resting
against the hard tabletop. Her mouth is half open, a thin
dribble running over the hand that had been propped
beneath her head, her neck twisted to the left.

The apartment is silent. Their mother has finally
fallen asleep. Sonja tries to look up at the clock on the
shelf over the kitchen table. In the pitch-darkness
she has to walk over, screw her eyes up, and tilt the face
in order to make out the hour. Half-past two. No sign
of Ilse.

Sonja had done her best to remain calm for as long as
Miriam had been awake. Ilse will be back soon, she
had said, she'll be back soon, just go to bed, it'll be fine.
She had recited an evening prayer with Miriam in
her bedroom, had heard the sound of her own voice,
her tone, the words flowing out of her much quicker
than usual and melting into one another, hard to
make out.

Their mother whispered to herself in the living
room. Round and round the table, over to the window,
into the kitchen, out into the hallway, always moving,
permanently accompanied by the never-ending sound
of her own muttering.

Sonja cleared the kitchen table after Miriam had gone to bed, carefully laying a yellow tablecloth with a white trim, fetching some side plates from the cupboard for breakfast the next day, giving herself something to do. Her mother came over, moved the side plates from the kitchen worktop, and started to lay the table, her hands shaking, the plates clinking together. It was a long time since her mother had laid the table, several weeks now. She tried to set the plates in neat symmetry, two on each side of the table.

"Do you think she's with Hermann?"

Her mother smoothed the tablecloth.

"She must be, don't you think?"

She hunched over the kitchen worktop. Sonja placed her hand on her mother's back, feeling her shallow gasps for air, her ribs jutting through her cardigan.

"I'll go over and ask the neighbors," she said. "Maybe they know something."

Her mother straightened up, stroking Sonja's hair.

"Go on, then," she mumbled, disappearing out into the living room.

It was past ten o'clock when Sonja knocked at the neighbors' door. Ingeborg opened up. Behind her, from inside the living room, she could hear Tinius's thundering voice.

"Shut the door, there's a draft."

Tinius was sitting in a green armchair in the farthest corner of the living room. There was a faint scent of cod-liver oil in the air, mixed with the smell of something fried, burnt.

"Ilse hasn't come home this evening," Sonja began. "She left this morning and didn't say where she would be going. Is Hermann at home?"

Tinius shook his head.

"So he could be out with Ilse, then?" Sonja ventured, half-questioning.

"You never know where Hermann is concerned," Tinius said. "He's here, there, and everywhere in the evenings. We guessed that he was with that snooty artist friend of his. He has a habit of staying over there. We can't tell him anything these days. He does what he wants."

Tinius glanced over at Ingeborg, who nodded slowly.

"But he didn't actually say he'd be with Ilse today?"

Sonja looked at Ingeborg.

"We haven't heard anything," she said quietly. "But we've both been at work all day and didn't get home until after six. There was nobody here when we got home. We're used to that, mind."

Tinius heaved himself up, a creaking sound coming from his chair.

"I hope Ilse comes back tonight," he said, placing a hand on Sonja's shoulder. "I really do. Young girls shouldn't be out in the middle of the night."

Ingeborg followed Sonja out into the hallway. She closed the door leading to the living room and moved in closer to Sonja.

"There were two fish cakes missing when we came home. Tinius doesn't know; he gets so irritated and you know what it's like with food these days. I just had to find something else for our dinner."

She hesitated for a moment.

"But maybe Hermann took one for Ilse," she continued. "He never usually takes more than he needs."

She looked long and hard at Sonja before closing the apartment door.

Sonja sits at the kitchen table hearing the ticking of the clock. Her neck aches, her mouth is dry, she feels uneasy after her dream. It's so dark in the apartment that she has to feel her way forward to avoid bumping into the furniture. She fumbles, hands outstretched, into the room where the sound of her mother's breathing is calm and easy, deep in sleep. Her hands find the edge of the bookcase that stands beside the door into the bedroom. She opens the door carefully, sneaking past Miriam's bed and lying down, still wearing all of her clothing. Her eyes stare out into the darkness of the room and she folds her hands, pressing them together firmly.

"Dear God, let Ilse come home tomorrow. Please God, don't let anything happen to her. Amen."

OLE RUSTAD IS NOT A MAN WHO LIKES getting up early. If he were in charge, he'd never start work earlier than ten; he needs time to get out of his bed and feel as if his body is holding together and his mind is clear, to make sure that the first words to come out of his mouth won't be the expletives he's been known to opt for after an all-too-short night's sleep. Things would be very different if Ole Rustad were in charge. If it were up to him, he'd have turned down the whole job, made it clear that meeting up on the opposite side of the city before the crack of dawn just wasn't right, that he didn't like being pushed around and told what to do as if he were a child. But Ole Rustad hadn't said anything of the sort. He had nodded at taxi chief Jørgensen, assured him that he'd be there, the taxi chief could count on him, he wouldn't go against an order, not an order like this. Plus, there was the money in it. They'd be paid well, that was for sure.

Ole Rustad turns off his alarm clock and peers out into the dark room. Anna is lying on her side; she's kicked off the eiderdown and her large stomach spills out toward the edge of the bed. He's told her that he needs to leave early, his taxi has been requisitioned for a job he doesn't know much about, but he'll be home again just after three, the job will probably be done by then. He's kept the rest to himself. Anna had fired a barrage of questions at him in a worried tone; was he getting himself involved in something, just before the baby was due? He had done his best to allay her fears, told her not to be afraid, promised that he would buy a new cradle with the money he expected to receive—a cradle and some clothes for the baby, maybe a coat for Anna and something for the girls too, some new dresses. She had smiled.

As he rolls out of the bed he can feel the blood pumping, his body feels like a pressure cooker, his vision goes black, and he has to sit for a few seconds on the edge of the bed until balance is restored. He feels queasy. His stomach grumbles.

He picks up the clothes lying on the chair by the side of the bed and gets dressed. His shirt smells sweaty, but he doesn't want to open the wardrobe to fetch a new one; doesn't want to wake the others, just wants to slip out of the house unnoticed and do what he has to until three o'clock, when he can return home once again.

He takes a look inside the bread box. There's half a loaf left; he removes it from its paper bag and holds it in his hands, bloody hell, it's so dry. He takes the cheese from the cupboard, slices off a chunk, it smells strong, sour, but there's nothing else. He stands in front of the mirror in the hallway with his bread and cheese in one hand and his coat in the other. Bloody hell, he looks exhausted, and it's so bloody cold too, God, he's looking forward to the day that all of this is over, once and for all.

He rummages around inside the bowl on the shelf beneath the mirror, finds the house key, the car key, opens the door, and closes it behind him carefully. A window in the stairwell has been left open, the cold wind blows in, a bitter November gust. He passes the door to the Sterns' apartment on the third floor, stops in his tracks, everything swirls around him for a moment all over again: the questions, the assurances he's given himself. There's not a sound to be heard. He carries on down the stairs.

After receiving the message to be there at half past four in the morning, they hadn't spoken much more about it. It was a message, no, more than that, it was an order, an order from the state police. Rolf was the only one who had said anything, though obviously not loud enough for anyone to hear, and not to the others, only to him when they had been alone for a few moments. Rolf had whispered, mumbled, just a few words, a snippet—Ole had only just managed to catch what he had said, and it was possible he hadn't heard him right. They hadn't been able to speak any more about it; the taxi chief had returned, nodded at them, and they had carried on with their work.

It is pitch-black outside and silent, nobody out and about at this time of day, the streets empty, deserted, even in the very center of the city. The insides of his nostrils sting as he inhales; there might be more snow today, he thinks, maybe it'll bring a little bit more light to the city streets, make it easier to get up in the mornings.

The windshield is covered in a thin layer of ice that he needs to scrape away. The cold nips at his hands; why the hell did he come out without his gloves? He looks at the clock: quarter past four, he's going to be late. Half past four, they'd said. Kirkeveien 23, he remembers the address.

The car starts the first time. He takes a right at the first crossroad, drives up Vogts gate and then turns left, picking up speed and cruising along Griffenfeldts gate, past the hospital and church and down toward Marienlyst.

He joins a swarm of other taxis, all on their way to the same address. Outside Kirkeveien 23 is a man in a police uniform, directing the vehicles here and there.

He waves his arms and blows his whistle; short, sharp blasts paired with quick, staccato gestures. Ole Rustad is directed to a parking spot where he turns off the motor and sits still for a second, observing the action taking place outside his window; everyone leaves their cars and walks in the same direction, nobody saying a word. There's something in the air, a friction, a certain nuance. They come creeping out of the night, trickling out of black cars and through alleyways; they can't be seen and nobody is allowed to know about them. Ole Rustad feels something tighten in his stomach, pressing on his left side, beneath his ribs, almost as if something is grasping at him, God, he feels sick. Should he restart the engine, back out of his parking spot, hurtle past the policeman, and charge back home, tell taxi chief Jørgensen that he had felt unwell—a blood clot, palpitations, unfortunately he couldn't make it after all? No, he can't do it. The money, he won't be paid, he's promised Anna the money, and he could be punished; it was an order from the state police after all, his taxi had been requisitioned. Why the hell did it have to be *his* taxi?

Ole Rustad had lingered in the stairwell when he had come home yesterday evening, overheard arguing from the Sterns' apartment, Ilse's voice, loud and filled with fury, Mrs. Stern. Should he knock at the door and tell them what Rolf had whispered to him? The Jews. But what if it wasn't true; how could Rolf know? He had said he *thought* that's what it was, suspected, but he didn't *know*, not for certain. Rumors ran rife these days. It was never-ending. Rolf always tended to think the worst, always so melodramatic, liked to make life that little bit more interesting, liked to be the one in the know.

Would it really be right to approach them with rumors, nothing but idle tittle-tattle, and to a family that was already in the midst of a crisis? Would that really be the right thing to do? And where would they go? If he were to knock at the door at this very moment in time, what then? He had no plan, but it wasn't as if they could just roam the streets. And Miriam, he had thought about her too, she often played with Karin, the two girls would sit and draw at the kitchen table together; could he really scare a child like that, create drama when it wasn't even necessary, kick up a lot of commotion for the whole family? What would they think if it turned out to be a false alarm; would they talk to him after something like that? He had stood in the stairwell and gone over all of it in his head as he had stared at their apartment door, contemplating his options, and then suddenly and without warning Ilse had come storming out. She had barely looked at him before running down the stairs, clearly upset about something. From inside the apartment he could hear Mrs. Stern crying and

Sonja's voice; he couldn't make out the words, only a sense of anxiety, confusion.

And then he'd gone. Up to his own apartment. He had closed the door behind him and convinced himself that he had done the right thing.

But now, sitting in his car and looking out the window in the brief moment before he became one man to join a stream of others, Ole Rustad can't help but ask himself one last time. He can sense his own unease, it thuds through him, blood, nausea. Someone knocks at his car window. There is a policeman outside. He leans down and looks inside, then makes a signal with his hand to indicate that Ole needs to get out of his car, something is beginning, something is already underway. Ole Rustad pulls the hand brake, opens his door, and steps out of the car. He is one of many now.

Standing in front of the crowd of drivers is a man in a police uniform, a megaphone in one hand. He discusses something with a man standing by his side, also in uniform. Ole Rustad glances around him, looking for anyone he knows, colleagues, Rolf. There are so many men there, hundreds maybe, all huddled tightly together. He recognizes a few of them, grave looks on their faces, nobody says a word, nobody laughs, everyone is exhausted, everyone is on guard, their eyes flicker from side to side looking for anything that might tell them what's going on, each of them looking for a sign. The air is sharp and cold, their faces shrouded by a frosty mist that lingers like a thick fog, emanating from silent mouths—a dense November haze escaping into the darkness of the night. Then the first sounds from the megaphone. Short commands. Clear instructions.

It's not long before Ole Rustad knows what the day will bring. Before long he's back in his car once again, though this time not alone—there are three others with him, a policeman in the front seat and two plainclothes officers in the back. Before long he drives his car back out onto Kirkeveien, back the very same way he had driven not that long ago. There is a glimmer of something else in the breaking daylight, a different chill in the air, as if he's driving around a foreign city, as if none of the streets are quite connected.

Before long Ole Rustad says nothing more that day. Not a single sound. He shifts gear, brakes, stops, starts, stares stiffly out the front of the vehicle and to the road, gripping the steering wheel firmly in both hands, never once turning to look at the backseat. He is silent.

SONJA IS WOKEN BY THE SOUND OF KNOCK-
ing. She sits upright, taking a second to come to
in the dark morning that envelops her. Can she
have been the only one to hear it? Was she dreaming, or
had she really heard a knock at the front door? The
alarm clock on the bedside table reads ten to six.
Miriam lies in bed facing the wall, the eiderdown pulled
right up around her so that only a little tuft of her hair
is showing. Their mother hasn't woken either. Sonja can
hear the sound of her mother's breathing from where
she lies in the living room.

More knocking. Louder this time. Three clear, insistent
raps; this isn't a dream.

"Sonja," her mother calls. "Sonja, did you hear that?"

Sonja is already up and out of her bed. She enters
the living room and lights the lamp on the wall by the
bookshelf, a narrow strip of light illuminating the
room, her mother's gray face and bloodshot eyes.

"It's Ilse!" Miriam cries out from the bedroom. "I knew she'd come home, I knew it!"

She leaps out of bed and scurries out of the bedroom and over to Sonja, lining up behind her in the hallway.

Another bout of knocking, more persistent this time, booming. Sonja presses her face up against the door.

"Ilse?"

No answer. Sonja turns the latch and opens the door that leads to the stairwell.

Three men are standing outside. One wears a police uniform, while the others are dressed in ordinary clothing, heavy winter coats, hats, scarves, sturdy boots. They stand huddled together, straight-faced, peering into the apartment.

"Mrs. Stern?" the man in the uniform inquires.

Sonja doesn't have a chance to reply before they force their way into the apartment, pushing through the front door and closing it behind them, speaking in hushed tones.

"Hell, it's so dark," the policeman grumbles. His voice is high-pitched, his features sharp; he quickly glances down at Miriam and strides into the living room. The other two follow him.

Sonja's mother is sitting up in bed. Her hair is disheveled, her mouth open, not a single muscle in her face moving. The man in the police uniform retrieves a handkerchief from inside his coat sleeve, blowing his nose and looking at the girls' mother.

"You need to leave," he says. "By order of the state police."

He stoops slightly and coughs, a long, hard, rasping hack, then uses his handkerchief to wipe around his mouth. He clears his throat once again and pulls out a sheet of paper. A heavy droplet hangs from the tip of his nose. It drips onto the paper he holds in his hand.

"Pack your things . . . the most essential items."

His voice is dry, the words whispered; he can barely speak. He hawks and splutters, his hacking cough resounding throughout the room. He passes the sheet of paper to the man by his side, points at it and makes his way into the kitchen, where he continues to cough. The man who remains is tall, dressed in a gray coat and large boots. He reads from the sheet of paper.

"Detainees will bring provisions to last four days: work clothes, footwear, underwear, woolen blankets, cups, plates, knives, forks, spoons, toiletries, any necessary medication, plus ration cards and identification documents."

He reads quickly, the words flowing into one another. He momentarily glances at their mother, at Sonja, then back down at the sheet of paper. He draws breath and continues.

"Use the best luggage you have, but nothing too large or bulky."

He stands for a moment, fiddling with the paper before folding it neatly. He doesn't look up.

It is quiet in the room. The policeman's latest bout of coughing subsides and he appears in the doorway, crossing his arms. Sonja looks at her mother. She sits motionless, her hands limp in her lap, no resistance in her body, no muscles. She almost appears not to be breathing. She looks at the floorboards, her gaze fixed on one point.

"Who needs to leave?" Miriam whispers to Sonja.

"All of you," the policeman replies in a thundering voice. "The whole family."

He wipes his nose again.

"Wear your warm clothes," he continues. "It's cold outside."

"Below freezing," mumbles the man in the gray coat.

Silence. Nobody moves an inch. They've been told to pack their things, to wrap up against the cold, they've been told that they need to leave but nobody flinches, they all stand stock-still. Their mother on the bed, Sonja and Miriam over by the table, the men in the living room doorway, all speechless for a few long, drawn-out seconds. It's so quiet that they can hear the ticking of the alarm clock in the bedroom, the sound of the crowded room, dense with bodies breathing in stale air; they can hear the tablecloth draped over the table, the books lining the shelves, the rug on the floor.

But then they hear something else. Their mother. She's laughing. She hunches her shoulders and opens her mouth. Loud laughter, a high-pitched bleating. They haven't heard her laugh for so long, nothing but the briefest chuckle for weeks now. There's been nothing to laugh about, nothing to smile about, for that matter. And now it rushes forth. Stockpiled sound.

The policeman looks around. He turns to the man by his side, shaking his head.

"Mrs. Stern?"

Their mother hears nothing. She sits on the bed in her nightgown and chortles to herself, mumbling, her mouth a gaping hole from which laughter continues to unexpectedly emerge.

The policeman looks at Sonja.

"Can you explain to me what exactly your mother finds so amusing about all this?"

Sonja looks at him, his eyes sharp with insistent questions, his pointed nose protruding from his face like a sharp beak. She walks over to her mother, sits beside her, and wraps her arm around her mother's back.

"Mum," she murmurs.

Her mother lies down, huddling beneath the eider-down, turning her back to the room and falling silent once again.

"Ilse," mumbles Miriam, still standing by the table. "What about Ilse?"

Sonja looks at Miriam, her gaze intense. Ilse. Should they tell the men that one of them is missing?

The policeman pulls out a piece of paper, unfolds it, and places it on the table.

"You are Sonja, yes?"

He splutters her name, dabbing around his mouth with his handkerchief and penciling an X by it when she nods.

"And you are Miriam Stern?"

Miriam nods. Another X on the piece of paper.

"And Hanna, over there."

He points his pencil in the direction of the body on the bed. Another hacking cough. He wipes his nose.

"According to my records there is an Ilse Stern miss-ing. Where is she?"

A grunt from the bed, not laughter, not tears, just a grunt. Sonja ponders the right thing to say, how best she might explain the situation. She doesn't have long to think.

"Answer me!"

He's there again, his eyes boring a hole in her, a look of impatience on his face. Sonja hesitates. The policeman signals to the two men to check the bedroom. They disappear into the room, their boots tramping on the floor. Sonja can see them pulling open the wardrobe, dragging items out and dropping them on the floor; one lies down to look under the bed.

"It is strictly forbidden to disobey an order from the state police," the policeman says. His high-pitched voice becomes squeakier, almost as if he's speaking in falsetto.

"Ilse isn't here," Sonja says.

"So where is she?"

The policeman glances back down at his piece of paper.

"She's fifteen years old, according to the information I have here. Why isn't she at home?"

"She went out yesterday and didn't come home."

It's Miriam who speaks up this time. She isn't looking at the policeman, but at Sonja.

"And you have no idea where she was going?"

"No."

The policeman jots something down. The pencil glides over the paper with speed and efficiency.

"This matter will be reported," he says. "I plan to follow this up personally. I'll make sure that she's found. I'll make sure . . ."

The men in the bedroom call out to him; they've turned the room upside down, clothes all over the floor, the mattresses half wrenched from the bed frames, bedsheets and pillows and blankets carelessly tossed in a pile. Sonja overhears snippets of the conversation in the next room, the men standing directly beside her bed.

"Shall we cross her off the list and say no more about it?" the man in the gray coat asks.

"Absolutely not," the policeman says. "Everything must be correct. Everyone on the list must be accounted for."

She can hear them discussing others they're due to call on later that same day. An older couple living on Seilduksgata; they wouldn't be much trouble, no madwoman there, no missing fifteen-year-old girls.

"You need to start packing," the policeman says as he emerges from the bedroom. "You don't have much time."

He's on his way out into the hallway, walking away from them when Miriam opens her mouth.

"Where are we going?"

He hesitates for a moment, wiping his nose and tucking his handkerchief back inside his coat sleeve.

"I won't discuss that further," he says, coughing and making his way toward the front door.

S ONJA STANDS MOTIONLESS FOR A MOMENT
after the door closes, bolt upright, silent, her gaze
fixed on the tabletop, her arms hanging limp by
her body, a rushing sensation filling her head. Ilse. Would
she have to return to an empty apartment? What is going
on? Where are they going? Her mother is still lying in
bed, her face turned away from everything that is
unfolding, no more than a backbone. She hasn't given
any indication of doing anything at all. She's said nothing, made no move, failed to even look at either of them.
She's not laughing anymore. She's not crying, whispering,
making a single sound. Miriam has gone into the bedroom. The man in the gray coat and big boots is sitting
in the kitchen keeping watch, making sure they don't do
anything they shouldn't, making sure they don't try to
run away. He hasn't said anything for a while either.

Packing. That's what she has to do. No matter what
they're heading for, they need to pack everything as
instructed, and it's down to Sonja to get on with it.

Into the kitchen. The man in the kitchen is sitting on a chair, leaning against the wall. The table is set and he sits at his place like an uninvited guest. Sonja finds a pan; they have eggs, four of them, she fills the pan with water and puts it on the stove, takes some bread from the bread box, places it on the kitchen bench, opens the cupboard door, takes out everything stacked inside. It's not much, certainly not enough to last them four days.

Out into the hallway. Coats, scarves, they've been told to dress warmly, she piles everything up on the living room floor. Back to the hallway, she fetches their boots, adds them to the pile. She works like a machine, automatic in her movements. Her arms and feet move instinctively, her mind planning her next move as if she's doing everyday household chores, washing, drying, moving, tidying. Packing.

"Something's boiling over here."

The man in the kitchen calls out to her in the hallway. Back into the kitchen, Sonja doesn't look at him; she finds the eggs, fetches a spoon, carefully lowers them one by one into the steaming water. She glances at the clock over the kitchen table, makes a mental note of the time, ten minutes, hard-boiled.

Into the bedroom. She has to find something they can pack their things in. They have a suitcase, the brown leather one, isn't it down in the cellar? Back into the kitchen. Steam rises from the stove; she can hear the eggs tumbling around inside the pan.

"Sorry, but I need to fetch our suitcase. It's down in the cellar."

She looks at the man seated at the end of the table, stares at him, questioning; it almost seems as if he doesn't know what she's talking about, he simply stares back at her, his eyes vacant, his mouth half open.

"May I go down to the cellar and fetch it?"

He closes his mouth. Furrows his brows. Looks long and hard at Sonja, as if considering her request, contemplating his response.

"No," he replies after a few moments. "You can't." He draws breath. "You'll need to find something else to pack your things in. You can't take much with you."

He reaches out to shift one of the side plates on the table, makes room for his elbow.

"Look, aren't those eggs done yet?"

Sonja glances at the clock. They've had fifteen minutes; she fishes them out of the water. She can feel him watching her, his eyes on her back. She works quickly, wants to get away from him, out of the room.

Their clothes are strewn over the bedroom floor, the mattresses cast aside. She opens the wardrobe door to find something to pack everything inside. Ilse's dress hangs there, the white one with the red spots; she lets her hand glide briefly over the thin fabric. On the floor of the wardrobe is something curled in a heap, a sack made of a coarse woolen fabric; she hasn't seen it in years. Sonja pulls it out and unfurls it.

Then she hears a sound from the bed.

"Miriam?"

She had forgotten about her, so preoccupied with getting everything in order, gathering their clothes and food, sorting things out when it seemed that nobody else would. Miriam is sitting on the bed. Has she been there all along?

"It'll be okay, Miriam," Sonja says.

Her tone is gentle. She sounds unconvincing even to herself, insincere.

"Really?"

Sonja nods, smiling at her.

"Do you know where we're going?" Miriam asks.

"I don't know."

Miriam looks at her long and hard.

"Maybe we're going on a holiday?" she says.

"Yes. It'll be a sort of holiday."

"Do you think we'll take the train?"

"Maybe."

"I want to sit by the window."

Sonja strokes Miriam's hair, tucking it behind her ears.

"You can. But for now you need to get yourself dressed."

Miriam hops off the bed and looks at the pile on the floor. She crouches down, finds her underwear and tights, and takes off her nightdress.

Sonja looks at her, her slender frame being gradually bundled up in layer after layer. She hasn't the time to watch Miriam now, they're leaving, but they don't know where they're going, Ilse isn't here, there's a strange man in a gray coat and heavy boots in their kitchen watching them as if they've broken the law. And Mum won't get up. Mum.

Out in the living room. Her mother's rapid, shallow breathing beneath the eiderdown.

"Mum?"

No reaction.

"Mum! You have to get up!"

And then he's there, swooping in without warning, the man from the kitchen. He lumbers into the room, stamping his boots, tearing away the eiderdown and throwing it on the floor.

"Get up!" he growls.

Her body is curled up in the fetal position, her arms wrapped around her legs.

"Move, you old bag! I've had more than enough of this, get up right now!"

Miriam emerges at the doorway, a sweater half pulled on.

"Go back to your room!"

Sonja's outburst is strict. She doesn't want Miriam to see this. But it's too late. Everything happens so quickly. The man grabs their mother with both hands and roughly pulls her up. Their mother is like a little girl in his huge arms, a mollusk. He sets her down on a chair, staring at her. She collapses, her body folding itself in two, her head falling forward.

"Move!" he says, before disappearing back out into the kitchen.

It is as if her mother is suddenly awake, as if she's been lying in a coma and is suddenly back with them. She sits straight-backed, glancing at Miriam and then at Sonja. She spits on the floor, a sizable gob, then stands up. Without making a sound or uttering a single word, she takes her clothes into the bedroom, pulls her nightdress over her head, and quickly dresses. When she's fully clothed she comes back into the living room. Her hands are back at work, her eyes alive; she moves around the room fetching things, placing them on the table, no longer whispering as she glides from one thing to the next. She stops by the bookshelf. Lingers there for a moment. She takes a picture frame, opens the back, removes the glass, and coaxes forth a photograph. All five of them smile in the picture, Ilse, a white ribbon in her hair.

Her mother disappears into the kitchen, where the man is sitting. Sonja can hear her speaking to him, her voice low; she can't hear what they're talking about, but the conversation doesn't last long. When she returns to the living room she places the photograph on the table, staring blankly into the distance.

Sonja crams everything into the coarse woolen sack. In the kitchen she finds a string bag, which she fills with everything she's placed on the kitchen work-top. The eggs have cooled slightly. She wraps them in brown paper and lays them carefully on top.

"The taxi's here."

The man with the boots is standing by the kitchen window. His tone is no longer angry; he's calmed down. They hear the sound of the front door and the police-man with the high-pitched voice appears once again. The man who has been keeping watch steps out into the hallway to greet him.

"Has everything gone to plan?" the policeman asks.

"Yes."

"And the woman? No longer laughing, I presume?"

"I made sure of it."

"Good," the high-pitched voice snarls.

Her mother and Miriam have put on their coats and

hats and Miriam is clutching her doll close to her. They stand in the doorway between the living room and hallway.

"You are to hand your key to me," the policeman says. "The apartment will be locked up until further notice."

He paces quickly around the living room and bedroom, checking everything is in order.

"Leave as quickly and as quietly as possible," he says, opening the door.

It is cold in the stairwell. The policeman locks the door behind them. Sonja hears the click as he turns the key. As they walk down the stairs, she slides her hand down the cold railing. A door bangs closed downstairs, snow covering the backyard. In the passageway it smells like winter. A black taxi is parked directly outside. The policeman opens the back door. Sonja turns around. The apartment block is dark and still. Behind the curtains on the third floor stands Ingeborg, barely visible.

They sit in the backseat with the sack and string bag between them. Their mother looks out the window while Miriam gazes at the driver. Straight-backed in the front seat, his hat is pulled down snugly over his head. He starts the engine, releases the hand brake, turns the steering wheel to the left, and the car rolls out onto the street.

H E CAN'T TURN AROUND. HE CAN'T HIDE
either. He is sure they've seen him, they must
have, he can feel their gazes on the back
of his head, he can sense the questions that hover in the
air between them. His right hand has started to tremble.
As long as he keeps a decent grip on the steering wheel,
it doesn't bother him, but as soon as he moves his hand
to the gear stick, as soon as he is required to do anything
other than steer, that's when it starts. He feels it travel
all the way from his shoulder and down through his
arm, an engine he can't switch off; he's shaking like an
old man, like a patient with some kind of critical illness.

Ole Rustad drives his car down Toftes gate, changes
gear, stops at the crossroad at Birkelunden Park, where
a woman in a green coat is crossing the road. Bloody
hell, she's taking her time, does it really take all day to
cross the road? He longs to use his horn, to blare it with
all his might, to roll down his window and bellow at her.

He drives on. The same route he had driven only a
short while ago.

It had been bad enough with the old folks down on Seilduksgata. He had driven the elderly couple down to Vippetangen not long ago while the Stern family had packed their things. They had sat in his car, man and wife, could have been in their seventies; the man had a walking stick and had been in real pain when he'd had to bend over and climb into the taxi. His wife had helped him, taking one of his legs and maneuvering it into place in the backseat before placing the stick on the floor of the vehicle and sitting next to him, wheezing slightly with each breath that she took. He had heard them speaking to each other, their voices low, whispering in a language he didn't understand; could it have been Russian? He hadn't turned around, hadn't spoken to them, but he had seen them in the mirror, both holding hands.

He tries to avoid looking in the mirror now, staring instead at the road in front of him. It's quiet in the car. He can hear his own breathing, short pants, like an animal. His shirt clings to his back, his hat strains at his temples. Why the hell is it just the three of them? He can't ask. He can't mention Ilse, can't let on to the policeman that he knows the passengers. So bloody queasy. Steering, changing gear, braking, stopping, that's all there is to it, that's all he can do, just transport his passengers from A to B.

They approach Vippetangen, quay number 1. He stops by the fence and turns off the engine. There are more people now than there were before, lines of them, the ship looming a few hundred meters away, towering and gray.

The passengers exit through the back doors of the car. They're carrying a thick woolen sack of some kind and a string bag, and they gather by the vehicle for a moment. He doesn't move a muscle. Can't turn around. Can't speak. What could he possibly say? What should he do? Pull them back inside the vehicle and drive off at full speed, past the men in the German uniforms? They would fire at his car, maybe even kill him in the process, or Mrs. Stern, or Sonja, maybe even Miriam. They wouldn't hesitate, not for a second; they'd use their weapons. He had seen what had happened with the walking stick, the way that one of the men in a German uniform had mocked the old man, laughed at him, taken his stick, snapped it in two and hurled it into the water. The old man had hobbled onward, leaning on his wife for support as a few of the guards whooped and called out to them. No, this wasn't the place to make a scene. Anyway, where would they have gone? Out of Oslo, into the countryside? He didn't know anyone who lived in the countryside, and they'd have been discovered sooner or later. Lilly and Karin would lose a father, plus Anna, and the baby on the way, he's thinking of them too, could he really leave them to fend for themselves? Where are they going, where are all of these people going? There must be a plan. It might not exactly be a holiday they were embarking on, but maybe it was better for them to take this ship wherever it was going than it would be to live as fugitives? They're probably being taken to a work camp somewhere; he's heard about these places. And they'll all be back, just as soon as things have calmed down a little.

A knock at his window. Miriam is standing outside. He sees her out of the corner of his eye, her red coat, her scarf, her hair. He sits in silence, staring straight ahead. His muscles are tense, but that bloody tremble, he can feel it in his legs now too. He can't turn around, can't roll down his window, can't wish her a safe journey. God-awful nausea.

"Drive on," says the policeman. "There are more names on this list."

Ole Rustad drives his car away from Quay 1. In his mirror he can see Miriam, Sonja, and Mrs. Stern as they make their way along the quay. His stomach rumbles, swirling like a drum rotating on its axis, the sweaty odor making him feel sick; he can't shake the question, it's all he can think about. Where the hell is Ilse?

THEY'VE ARRIVED, AND THE SHIP BOBS on the waves in the harbor basin, slowly up and down, a floating gray block, letters on the prow: *Donau*.

"Are we going by boat, Sonja?"

Miriam's voice is quiet, almost a whisper. She holds Sonja's hand, clutching her doll close to her with her free hand.

"I think so."

"But you said we'd be taking the train. You said I could sit by the window."

"And you can. If we take the train."

"Sonja?"

"Yes?"

"How long will we be on the boat for?"

"I don't know, Miriam."

"Sonja?"

"Yes?"

"Will Ilse be here soon?"

Sonja hesitates, thinks things over; how can she answer that question? She has always tried to answer Miriam's questions, even when she knows very little herself, tried to be calm, to act as if nothing is going to harm them, that everything will be just fine. But now. Here. The quayside is packed with people, coats, hats, caps, kids — many are crying, two old people cling to each other, a woman in a fur coat holds a baby in her arms wearing a little red hat. Suitcases, bags — people's belongings strewn everywhere, some people sitting on their luggage — the noises, loud, scraping.

A little boy in a blue woolly hat turns around and looks at Miriam. He's holding hands with a woman in a white shawl standing with her back to them, but when she turns around Sonja can see that her belly protrudes from her open coat. She says something to the boy, pointing at the suitcase that lies next to them. The boy looks down, disappears for a moment in the throng of people, and then reappears. He looks at them, Miriam, curiosity lighting up his face, then scrunches up his eyes and sticks out his tongue. Miriam hasn't seen him; she's too busy looking up at Sonja. Sonja can tell that she wants an answer to her question, but what can she possibly say, there is no answer, she can't say what she fears to be true: They'll be leaving without Ilse.

Miriam's cold fingers holding Sonja's hand, squeezing tight, tugging at her.

"Sonja?"

"I'm going to look for Ilse," Sonja says. "Maybe she's somewhere around here. Stay here. I'll be back soon."

The guard, he'd hit their mother with a rubber club when she hadn't been able to explain Ilse's absence at the checkpoint. They'd had to tell them everything, and everything they said had to match the information on the list, but there was one thing that wasn't there, yet should have been; a large hole they couldn't fill, questions they had no answer to. The guard was young, not much more than twenty perhaps, an acute glint in his eyes, on the prowl; he measured them up as he gazed at them, green uniform and black boots, German. He approached their mother, stood directly before her; she didn't flinch, only looked down, gripping the sack tightly. There was a long silence. His breath in their mother's face. And then suddenly, without warning, he had screamed in her ear: *"Judenschwein!"* When her mother was sure he had finished she made an error of judgment. She lifted her head and met his gaze, for a brief moment looking him directly in the eye. Then there he was with the club. Quick as a flash he pulled it from his belt, lifted his arm, and brought it down across her face. Their mother fell forward, holding her forehead, blood trickling between her fingers. Miriam wailed. The guard turned around and gave a signal to the man at the checkpoint that they could carry on, he was done with them. He returned the club to his belt and walked over to the two other men in green uniforms, took a packet of cigarettes from his pocket, and offered it to the others as they chatted and laughed together.

Sonja looks at them, her mother with her handkerchief, Miriam with her doll. They say nothing to one another. Her mother unfolds the handkerchief to find a clean spot to hold to her wound, pressing the fabric to her head.

What had Ilse been wearing when she'd run out the door the previous day? Brown coat, lace-ups, white wool hat. The crowd huddles together; Sonja goes from one person to the next asking if anyone has seen a young girl, all on her own, wearing a brown coat, a wool hat; she whispers the words. A woman with three children gathered around her points.

"She's over there," she says. "Over by the sick people."

Sonja feels a stabbing sensation within. The sick people. Sonja hasn't come across any sick people, not yet. But now, as she turns around, she can see stretchers being carried in. She doesn't know quite what she hopes to find, whether it's hope or fear that rises within her; she can't work out what she sees.

A girl stands there with her back to Sonja. A brown coat and a wool hat, she's all on her own, a few meters from a family sitting on two suitcases, motionless, like a statue that has been erected in the middle of the quay. Sonja runs, blood pumping through her body, forgetting for just a moment where she is, that she has to be careful, the guards in green uniforms, she mustn't attract attention.

"Ilse," she shouts, she knows she mustn't shout but she can't help herself. "Ilse!"

The girl stands still. There's just a few meters between them. Then she turns around abruptly.

She's younger than Ilse, perhaps no older than thirteen. Her hair hangs down by her face; she's pale, with large black eyes, her mouth forming something close to a smile.

"Are you looking for someone?"

Sonja says nothing. She bends over, gasps for air, sits on her haunches for a moment and stares at the ground. She can see the girl's shoes, the tips of them pointing right at her, immobile. For a second Sonja is so small, twelve years old, eleven maybe, younger than the girl before her, younger than she remembers being in a long time. She opens her mouth, goes to say something, but no sound comes out. She wants to tell the girl that she thought she was Ilse, to tell her that Ilse has gone missing, how afraid she is for her—she wants to tell her about her mother, sitting on the sack and dabbing at the blood on her face, about Miriam who never stops asking questions, about the neighbor who had driven them here, the way he had pretended not to know them. She wants to tell her everything. But there's so much commotion, an infant howls shrilly, metal against the hard ground, orders being called out, a man wails, he calls out a name just a few meters away, he's lying on a stretcher; Gerda, he groans, Gerda. Everything moves as if through a filter, all the contours fade to transparency, only sediment remains all around her, everything distorted. She remains crouched down, can't face standing up again, her legs ache but other parts of her too, even more so. Her mother and Miriam can't see her here, they're sitting too far away, there are hundreds of bodies between them. She's alone for a moment, just a moment before she has to return to them, and in that moment it all floods forth; everything she's held in, hidden from Miriam, hidden from her mother.

When she looks up again the girl is gone, as if she'd never been there in the first place. Sonja looks around to see where she has disappeared to, but she fails to spot her anywhere.

Her legs tingle. She makes her way over to where her mother and Miriam are sitting, stopping as she catches sight of them. Miriam is sitting with a boy, the one wearing the blue hat who had stuck his tongue out at them not so long ago. Now the boy is huddled close to Miriam with her doll in his lap. Sonja sees Miriam showing him how to remove the doll's sweater by undoing the buttons at the back.

"Erik's learning how to dress Bella," Miriam says as Sonja walks toward them. The boy's hands twist and turn around the doll, taking off her sweater and skirt and looking at the naked doll's body with a satisfied expression.

Sonja says nothing, standing and looking at them, but then she catches Miriam's gaze and it is as if Miriam has suddenly remembered why she is there, as if she has only just noticed that Sonja has returned alone.

"I couldn't see Ilse," Sonja says before Miriam has the chance to ask.

Then something happens. Several people move, stand up, look at the fence. It is as if the crowd holds its breath, a collective hush falling over the throng of people. They come in flocks, streaming onto the pier, a rush of bodies. And there, at the front, it's him, it's definitely him.

ONJA'S FACE IS THE FIRST THAT ISAK SEES.
Her red hat, gray coat, the scarf around her
neck, when she's bundled up in so many layers
her face looks so small, but even so he knows that it's
her. He can see her eyes, looking right at him, filled
with questions; has she seen that it's him, does she
recognize him? It feels as if a thousand days have passed
since he saw her last. So much has happened in these
past few weeks, so many thoughts have passed through
his mind, so much fear, so much hope. This is exactly
what he has hoped for and exactly what he has feared.
That he would see them again. That it would be here.

She raises her hand in a kind of wave, yes, she waves
at him, she's seen him. He lifts his left hand, his right
fist clenched. His fingers all still stinging, he can feel
them throbbing, the pain pumping steadily beneath his
nails, yellow and thick. Now he can see Hanna too, she
stands up, just behind Sonja, he can see that she's holding something white, pressing it to her head. Sonja lifts

Miriam, points, Miriam's head turning, her eyes desperately searching.

The joy at seeing them again swells inside him, regardless of the situation; he's been so afraid that it would never come to pass, that he'd never get through it, never come out alive.

He had tried to have a letter smuggled out to them. One evening in the barracks he'd found a pencil stub on the floor, picked it up, hidden it, and every day he had hunted for something that he could use, a scrap of paper, anything at all that he could scribble a few words on; just so they'd know where he was, that he was alive. And one day there it was, hanging before him, a written order to the prisoners pinned to the wall with a drawing pin. It said something about lice, the need to be mindful about personal hygiene, but the text covered only the top half of the sheet of paper. That same night he fumbled his way over to the piece of paper, pulled out the drawing pin, and hid the sheet beneath his thin mattress. He ripped off the lower half and wrote a message during the night in the pitch-darkness. The morning after, when he saw what he'd written, he realized that it looked like something scribbled by a six-year-old. The letters were lopsided and childish, and at some points he'd missed the mark entirely and the words merged into one another. But it was possible to read three sentences:

All is well. At Berg near Tønsberg. Home soon. He couldn't be certain about the last bit, but he wanted to give the impression of being in control of the situation, that he had heard news, that he'd soon be back.

He'd noticed one of the prison guards, a young man with a distinctive western accent. He wasn't as short-tempered as the others, never threw insults around or became violent with them. There was something in his eyes, in the way that he looked at the prisoners, as if he didn't wish to torment them any further. His colleagues did all that they could to humiliate and bully them, showing off their own strength while the young man stood in the background, silent. Maybe he hadn't realized what the work would entail, Isak thought, maybe he was just glad to have found something to do; he was young and no doubt needed the money, just like everyone else.

One evening an opportunity arose. The young prison guard stood at the top of the barracks to take watch, making sure the men turned in for the night. As usual he stood without saying a word, gazing vacantly ahead, no commando cries, not a sound to be heard from him. Isak approached, his hand clasping the piece of paper in the pocket of his prison outfit; he had folded it up and written the address on the outside. He was taking a huge risk, he'd seen the way that the guards had reacted to people even over the most trivial things: taking too long at mealtimes, a missing button on their uniforms, an answer that didn't come quickly enough for their liking. They'd had to experience it. And now there he stood, trying to deliver a piece of paper.

The prison guard looked at him, yes, what did he want? Isak kept his gaze low, could he go to the toilet? The prison guard nodded; Isak glanced up for a brief second and looked him in the eye.

"Please," he whispered, holding out his hand.

The prison guard snatched the piece of paper, a lightning reflex, his eyes flashing.

Isak broke into a cold sweat that night, lying in his bed and picturing Hanna's face, her smile, perhaps even her tears as she read those three lines and called for the girls.

The following day, the guard failed to turn up. Another guard stood and watched them, the kind who loved the job and the sound of his own boots patrolling the bunks.

His anxiety about seeing them again, the uncertainty. The men had talked about it on the train that very morning. Tightly huddled in the carriage, he'd heard several of them wondering aloud if they'd ever see their families again. It hadn't been an optimistic conversation — quite the contrary, in fact. The notion that they might trundle into Oslo and be permitted to go their own ways seemed improbable; nobody really expected it to be the case, not after a month spent at Berg.

They hadn't received any word about where they were going, though many believed they might be headed to a work camp in the north of the country. If they were to see their families that day, then it could only mean that they were being sent away too.

And now, as they arrive at the quay, he feels the questions swirl around inside him like dry leaves. Where are they going? All these people. What's going on? He sees the ship, the confusion of suitcases, the guards in green uniforms, hears the shouts, the cries of children, the drone of the vessel. It doesn't bode well, he's certain of it. He might have thought, once or twice, in spite of everything that had happened, that things could turn around, get better. But now he's seen too much, heard too much. They are going to die. He knows it.

He waves at Miriam, who smiles at him. Just a few meters now, a few meters separating them. But then he realizes; she isn't there. Ilse isn't with them.

THEY HOLD EACH OTHER CLOSE. HE buries his face into her neck, feels her cold skin against his nose. Hanna doesn't smell the same, not the way that he's used to. She smells of sweat; he becomes aware of the odor of her body. He's always felt that their bodies fit perfectly together, but now she's so thin, on the brink of disappearing. He can feel her trembling slightly, a faint shake, as if her legs might give way beneath her at any moment. He squeezes her hard, moves his left hand up to her face, and holds her like a newborn baby that can't quite lift its own head yet.

"Ilse?" he whispers in her ear. "Why isn't Ilse here?"

He releases his grip on her and looks her in the eye. He's never seen her looking so anguished, so completely distraught. She doesn't respond to him, just looks at him, her lips thin, dry, her eyes cloudy. Blood trickles from a long cut above her right eye; somebody must have hit her hard. She sinks down onto the rough woolen sack and presses a handkerchief to her fore-head; he can hear her groaning.

Isak hugs Miriam, lifting her up and holding her close, her body hanging in his arms. He feels her breath, a warm tickle against his cheek, her lips.

Sonja, the one he'd seen first. Her eyes are red and puffy.

"Do you know where we're going?" she whispers as they embrace each other.

"No," he replies, looking around. "I don't know."

He can sense her unease, her eyes flickering all around.

"Where is Ilse?" he asks; he still hasn't received an answer.

"We don't know," Sonja says. "She didn't come home last night."

He can't say what he's thinking, that perhaps it's a good thing that Ilse isn't there, that perhaps she's been lucky. He can't say it, can't give too much away. He has to keep his assumptions to himself, everything he fears, none of it can be allowed to slip out.

Hanna is standing once again.

"Where have you been, Isak?"

She stares at him.

The letter; he knows now that they never received it,

that Hanna hasn't known where he's been since the moment he walked out the door that morning, one month ago. He hesitates, doesn't quite know where to begin. He doesn't have the time to go into detail, doesn't wish to either, not here, not now. She's troubled enough as things stand, her face is so gaunt, her skin almost transparent. He has to choose his words carefully now, say only what's necessary, just as he had in the letter he had written that night. He thinks for a brief moment.

"I've been at Berg detention center, near Tønsberg," he says.

He feels the dull ache in his bad hand; it throbs. He gives her a wary smile. Inhales.

"I'm just fine, don't you worry," he adds.

H E'S NOT FINE. HE HASN'T BEEN FINE for a long time. He can still feel the cold mud that they'd had to roll around in, the way that their uniforms had become rigid after standing for hours in the square where they held roll call. He still has the taste of rotten turnip in his mouth from the soup they were fed, and he can still hear screams, some of them his own, from when they had laid into his right hand.

He didn't know where he was going when they had come to arrest him that morning. It was dark outside and no later than six o'clock; he was flanked by two men who didn't speak to each other. They took the tram to Majorstua, walked in the direction of Frogner Park, and stopped at Kirkeveien, just outside number 23. Once there he had been required to register and they wanted to know everything: his name, date of birth, address, profession, nationality, height, weight. There were other men there when he arrived, the youngest aged sixteen and others of all ages above that, and all Jewish. He recognized several of them.

They were ordered to stand in a line with their faces to a brick wall, lifting their arms above their heads. They waited. Isak closed his eyes, listened, footsteps, voices; he was going to die, he thought, there, with his arms in the air, shot against a wall. By his side was a man, around thirty maybe, beads of sweat forming on his forehead, his arms shaking.

How long had they stood there? It had felt like hours. Isak felt the prickling sensation in his arms, all the blood pooling at his shoulders, his shoulder blades thumping, his neck burning. Heavy-duty vehicles trundled into the area. They were ordered to board buses and trucks, all with their arms still held above their heads.

Through Oslo and out of the city, heading eastward, there was silence on board. A dark building appeared before them as the bus drew to a halt. Bredtveit Prison. It rained. Isak squeezed his eyes tight shut, felt the droplets run from his hairline and down over his forehead; they stood in line for a long time, the guards shielded from the downpour by umbrellas. Roll call; everyone was to be entered into the prison register, address, profession, date of birth, the same information all over again. Then one by one they were taken to a room where men in white coats were required to perform a brief medical examination.

The following morning they were ordered to march down the hillside in front of the prison toward an empty train that waited on the tracks; the guards called out to them that they had to make haste, they needed to run, and they bumped into those who dawdled, pressing themselves tightly into the carriages to allow the doors to close and the train to leave.

They arrived at Berg detention center that evening, which was situated deep within a dense forest. Barbed wire surrounded the center, eleven or twelve guards standing in a semicircle as they marched in the door. There were some low buildings around the open main square, large floodlights. On that first night they slept on the floor. Isak had been allocated a space beside a man he had met at Kirkeveien, Samuel, who trembled where he lay.

He looks Hanna in the eye. He's never done that before, lied to her face. He may have embellished the truth once in a while, carefully chosen what to share with her, but this is a lie; he's told her he's fine but it couldn't be further from the truth. She looks at him, a long, hard gaze. She doesn't believe him, he can tell. She has that look he knows so well, the one that bores its way deep inside him and sees what he can't bear to see himself. He feels his hand, heavy, swollen, distended.

The sausage. He had stolen it from the kitchen. Gnawed and gnawed at the meat, the salty flavor spreading through his mouth—he hadn't thought twice, had simply reached out a hand and grabbed it. Three weeks of turnips from the large pans of soup, the sausage was for the employees, yet still Isak sat on the latrine and chewed.

The following day the missing item was noticed. For a number of hours they stood lined up as the guards walked from one end of the line to the other. If nobody admitted to this, they'd take ten men from the lineup, it could be any of them, the guards told them as they passed. Isak shook, sweated, he ought to say something, confess, ten men, he kept his mouth shut, looked down at the ground. A guard approached him, stopped in front of him, and stared at him for several minutes.

"Isn't this the kitchen helper?" he said after a few moments. "Isn't this the turnip chief? The esteemed soup chef?" he continued, mockingly.

Isak didn't lift his gaze, he knew the rules; if the guards asked them something then they were to look down, not at them.

"You're in the kitchen every day," the guard continued. "Do you have something you want to tell us?"

They had marched him into a room in the guards' quarters. Ten strokes on his right hand. After the fifth he no longer registered when the cane met its target. Only that evening as he lay in the barracks had he seen how bad the damage was. The nails of his index and middle finger were crushed, a flesh wound spanning his entire hand. He groaned where he lay that whole night, throwing up on the floor in a state of semiconsciousness.

Green uniforms swarm the pier, shouting over one another, barking orders, shoving people aside. He hears people begging for themselves and their families, begging to be allowed to leave. One woman's clothing has been ripped almost to shreds and she tries her best to cover herself, her body exposed, holding her arms over her naked breasts. He can see Miriam clutching on to Sonja, gazing all around her, saying nothing.

The air brims with activity, dense with fog and steam. Something is happening. The time has come for the passengers to board.

THEY MAKE IT BACK BY THE MORNING, Ilse Stern and Hermann Rød. The tram journey down from Kjelsås feels so long, the city coming into view atop the Grefsen plateau, the tenements down below, three people sitting in one of them, waiting, anxious, fearful. Hermann sits by her side. He looks serious. She moves closer to him, rests her head against his shoulder; he smells so good, so safe, she could sit here all day, just like this, in silence at his side. The tram stops at Torshov, the doors opening up once again, humming, she places her hand on Hermann's; his hand is warm, the cut now dry and hardened, a dark red stripe on his index finger. He had broken the glass with nothing but his bare hands, squeezing his body through the narrow windowpane and breaking into the cabin. What would she say; how would she explain it when she got home? She looks at Hermann and he smiles at her, hesitant, maybe not a smile after all, just his lips moving. Yesterday she had only intended to walk and walk, all through the city and then back home in the evening after having made her mother sit and stew. But now, now she'd spent the whole night away, she hadn't planned on staying out for so long. The tram trundles toward Biermanns gate. She would have to embellish the truth slightly, make things sound much worse than they had been, exaggerate a little. The darkness, the snow, the empty cabin they'd just *had* to break into, the cold, the fear, how lost they had been. It's not possible to explain, she's gone too far now, her mother is bound to fly off the handle, unleash all the thoughts that have plagued her since Ilse's disappearance, and she deserves it this time; defending herself isn't an option.

"Hermann?" she says, as they alight the tram. "Can you come in with me? Please?"

Silence in the stairwell. Ilse opens the door down to the cellar, holds her skis under her arms, and makes her way down the steep staircase. She can see the benches in the half darkness; it's cold down there, damp. Ilse props her skis up against a wall and removes her pitch-seam boots, then finds the shoes she had on yesterday. Time to get it over and done with, up to the third floor, into the apartment; time to explain, time to take what's coming her way.

They stand outside the apartment door for a moment in silence. Two closed doors leading to each of their apartments. Not a sound to be heard. Hermann has removed his hat, his hair falling across his forehead, tousled. Suddenly she feels the urge to lean in, to kiss him, he loves her, he had said it himself, that night up in the cabin; love, but it's not the time, not here, not now. She grasps the handle, pushes it, leans her body weight against the door. The door is locked.

She stands for a moment and looks at Hermann. Are they out looking for her? She can picture them, up and down the city streets, afraid, they might have been out all night. Poor Mum, she must have been out of her mind with worry; Ilse had never stayed out all night before, she'd come back late, yes, but she'd always come back. Her head throbs. She tries once more, pushing the door with all of her weight, knocking, hard, frantic, pressing her ear to the door and listening keenly. Silence.

Then the door to Hermann's apartment opens. Ingeborg sticks her head out. She fixes her gaze on them and quickly ushers them inside, her index finger to her lips, glancing around the stairwell.

"Mum," Hermann utters with surprise. "Shouldn't you be at work?"

Ingeborg shepherds them into the living room. She doesn't say a word, just stands opposite them. Hesitates.

"You can't be here," she says, looking at Ilse. "He

could come back any minute." She speaks in hushed tones, her voice shaking slightly.

"Who are you talking about, Mum?"

"The policeman," Ingeborg whispers to Ilse. "He's looking for you."

They stand in the living room, all three alert in a close circle. They know that they need to get moving, that time isn't on their side, but it is as if they have frozen, unable to move any farther. Ingeborg has told them what she saw. She doesn't know anything, she says, doesn't know where they're going or when they're coming back, but she tells them exactly what she saw, exactly what she heard. Early this morning she'd been standing at the window as they had climbed inside a taxi. Ingeborg draws a deep breath.

"There was a policeman here not long ago; he has the apartment keys. I heard him let himself in. I'd imagine it's you he's looking for."

Ilse says nothing, staring at Ingeborg. She can't get her head around all that she's heard, can't make any sense of the words that have come out of Ingeborg's mouth; just words, swirling around in the air between them, circling them like insects that she can't catch.

"You can't be here," Ingeborg repeats. "Do you have somewhere that you can go?"

The cabin. There was a stove there, and they'd found

wood and lit a fire, curled up on the floor, huddled together, last night had been so good, but now, suddenly, this.

"I know what to do." Hermann looks at Ingeborg. "I know someone."

Ingeborg looks at him, her eyebrows furrowing to form two straight lines.

"Don't do anything stupid," she says.

"I won't, Mum. You have to trust me. I know where we can go."

The cabin. Is that what he's talking about, is he going to come with her? She can't ask, can only hope.

"Can you help me with something?" he asks his mother, continuing before she has the chance to respond. "Can you find some clothes? Wool stockings, a shawl, a coat if you have one, some food. And money. Do you have any lying around?"

Ingeborg stands before him without saying a word, her mouth half open, her lips dry, then makes her way into the kitchen and opens a drawer.

"Hermann," she calls after a moment. He follows her into the kitchen.

Ilse stays where she is, still and silent. Hermann and his mother converse in low voices in the next room.

"I can't tell you," she hears Hermann tell his mother. "No, Mum. You just have to trust me. I know what I'm doing."

"What about you?" Ingeborg asks. "Are you coming back?"

"Yes. I'll be back. I promise."

The cabin, it can't be the cabin, Hermann can't leave her up there on her own, the lump in her stomach, it throbs, where have they gone, where are they going? Her heart thumps harder and harder within her rib cage, faster and faster; it is as if the sound drowns out all others, piercing the silence of the room, forcing its way into the kitchen, where Hermann assures his mother that he knows what he's doing, it goes on and on and on, hammering and hammering. Then very suddenly a different sound. A rattling from the stairwell. Unmistakable. The sound of someone letting themselves into the neighboring apartment.

Ingeborg stops in her tracks in the kitchen. She stands unflinching, bread knife in hand. She moves her index finger to her lips and stares into the living room, as if to make sure that Ilse understands; there is nobody at home. Ilse stands motionless, barely breathing. She hears someone moving around in the apartment next door, footsteps, a hacking cough, voices, the bang of the door once again, the click of the lock. Footsteps down the stairs. But Ilse knows those stairs so well. She can distinguish between the sound of footsteps going down and footsteps coming up. Somebody is making their way back up the stairs.

There's a knock at the door. Four short, decisive raps of a knuckle. They don't move. Ingeborg has placed a hand on Hermann's shoulder, gripping him tight, the bread knife in her other hand.

More knocking.

"Anyone home? This is the police."

A high-pitched voice, almost like that of a woman.

A hand on the door handle. She hears it moving up and down several times. Ingeborg closes her eyes.

Then footsteps, this time going down the stairs. The gate out onto the street closes with a loud clang.

They remain in the same positions for a good while after the sound of the footsteps has faded, three statues sculpted at opposite ends of the apartment. Hermann is the first to move. He enters the living room, approaches Ilse, and strokes her hair quickly before creeping over to the windows. He walks sideways like a crab on the seabed, avoiding detection. He stands behind the curtain, leaning just far enough that he can see down onto the street below, then quickly pulls back and walks away from the windows.

"They're waiting outside," he whispers.

———

When they emerge again a few hours later, they are greeted by blinding white light. The snow has melted in the city, leaving behind nothing more than a fine layer of frost in the backyard, the branches of the lilac tree reaching upward, black against the white sky. Ilse can hear the sound of her own footsteps as she passes the rubbish bins and walks out of the front gate. Out on the street she turns around to look at the gray tenement building, the apartment windows, kitchen, living room, darkness within. It looks so quiet.

She places one foot in front of the other, her shoes against the asphalt, turning away from the building, can't think too much, just has to walk, to move on.

They walk toward the Akerselva River, crossing Beier Bridge. The waterfall has frozen, with only a few trickles dripping from the large yellow-white mass of ice. They walk past the weaving mill, several factory workers on their breaks congregating in small groups out in the square where they smoke and laugh together.

Over Iladalen and up Geitmyrsveien, Hermann takes her hand, onward through Bislett, he hasn't told her where they're going, who they're going to see, she hasn't asked either, they just walk. Josefines gate, over Hegdehaugsveien, Frogner, the large apartment buildings lined up in neat rows, soft facades and small front gardens, the wind blows, it's so cold outside.

HERMANN RINGS THE BELL, THREE SHARP trills, then leads Ilse into the expansive hall-way and up the stairs. She hasn't asked him where they're going, where they are, she hasn't uttered a single word since they left his apartment. Einar's expression is grave when they reach the fourth floor, standing in the doorway, smoking, looking at them both. Hermann ushers Ilse in first, then closes the door behind them.

"The young Miss Ilse Stern," Einar says, a fleeting, hesitant smile crossing his lips, but stops himself, as if he already knows exactly why they've come.

"Do you have spa—"

Einar nods before Hermann has the chance to finish his question. "There's space," he says. "You can have the red room."

They walk down the long hallway, it is dark inside his apartment today; the door to the yellow room is closed. Einar opens the door to the red room and nods at Ilse, she stops, looks around her; the curtains are drawn, his glass from Tuesday night still sitting on the bedside table, a splash of dried brandy at the bottom.

"You'll have to stay here until further notice," Einar says. "Keep away from the windows and be as quiet as you can. The neighbors are almost deaf, but you never know." He smiles. "It can take some time, a few days maybe, but we'll get you across."

Ilse looks at Einar, then at Hermann. He has to explain, she doesn't understand, he can see it in her eyes, the way she stands there, speechless.

Einar nods at Hermann, then asks him to join him in the kitchen.

"I'll be back soon," Hermann says. Ilse stays where she is, motionless in the middle of the room, yet to remove her coat.

"Why only Ilse?" Einar asks, pulling out a kitchen chair and sitting down.

Hermann opens his mouth to explain.

"An operation was carried out throughout the city today," Einar continues. "I heard about it only an hour ago."

He stubs out his cigarette in an ashtray, ripples of smoke curling upward. "I expected there to be more of them." Einar fixes Hermann with a scrutinizing gaze. What the hell is he supposed to say, squirming before

Einar; he should have said something yesterday, last night, no, long before that. He can help Ilse across, but the others; he had chewed over the information he had for so long, he had been so quiet, what the hell was he thinking?

Hermann turns and walks out of the kitchen. Ilse is sitting on the bed. He closes the door and sits down beside her. Her hair smells of smoke. The cabin, her face in the dim room, they'd huddled close to each other, he hasn't slept all night. He could have managed to find his way back to the city, he hadn't been quite as lost as he'd made out. It had been so good, a long break, a set of parentheses around all of his secrets, Ilse Stern and Hermann Rød. Let tomorrow come, he'd thought, feeling Ilse's hair brush his cheek, let it come, as it is. The crackling from the stove, the cold, the peace he'd felt, those few hours they'd had together before everything would go back to how it had been; he couldn't know what the hell tomorrow would bring.

Ilse looks at him.

"Where am I going?" she asks.

"You have to go to Sweden."

He sees her swallow; the notion can't have occurred to her before now, this is news to her, they obviously hadn't discussed it at home, Sweden, he could have said anything, Siberia, the South Pole, she looks confused.

"Can you come with me?"

She whispers, looking away.

He strokes her hand with his index finger, then cups her cheek with his palm.

"You know that I can't, Ilse."

She nods.

"Ilse Stern," he whispers softly in her ear.

"Will I see you before I go? Can you come back here?"

"I'll try to come tomorrow," Hermann says.

He takes off his wool sweater, folds it, and places it on the bed.

"It gets cold," he says.

Her cheek, her lips, the muscles in her arms, she holds him close. He has to go now, he has to leave, alone, he squeezes her tight. Stands up. Closes the door and walks away.

B
Y THREE O'CLOCK OLE RUSTAD IS DONE
for the day. Finally he can drive home, park his
taxi, go up to his family, change his shirt, eat
his dinner, play with Lilly and Karin and let Anna get
some rest.

But he doesn't. Not straightaway.

He revs the engine as it hums uphill, changes gear,
brakes, steers, and turns. He doesn't stop until he reaches
Ekeberg Hill. He climbs out of the car. Draws the
cold air deep into his lungs. He's been here many times
before; it's a beautiful spot. The view over the city, the
houses so small, like matchboxes, the cars, the traffic,
like insects, all the way down below. He can see the
ship just off Nesoddlandet. It glides out into the fjord.

It's so still out there. Everything looks so peaceful.
The trees sigh. Yellow leaves are scattered over the
frosty grass, dry and stiff. A pile of leaves rustles as
he kicks it. When he turns to the right, he can see all the
way home. Far off in the distance he can see the Ringnes
brewery. He can see the tenement on Biermanns gate,

squeezed in between the others on the block. It feels like an eternity has passed since he left that morning. Anna sits there waiting for him, and the new baby, it wouldn't be long now, it could be a boy or a girl, it's all the same, really.

Bloody nausea. Bloody body odor. He looks at his hands, holds them in front of his face, the right hand still trembling.

He thinks about all that he has heard, all that was said in the car. The policeman with the high-pitched voice who had been sitting in the passenger seat, speaking to one of the others, the one who had taken guard duty in the Sterns' apartment.

"I've got a name," the man in the backseat had said.

"A what?" The policeman turned and looked at his colleague, his seat creaking.

"The madwoman," the man in the back continued. "She came to me in the kitchen and gave me a name."

Ole Rustad stopped at a junction, his eyes lingering on the mirror.

"Hermann Rød," the man in the backseat said. "The old bag reckoned the girl might be with this Hermann Rød. He lives on the same floor."

The policeman took a note of the name on a piece of paper and smiled.

"Is that so," he mused.

Ole Rustad looks out over the fjord, his stomach tight, grumbling furiously. He paces back and forth, can't calm himself down, can't get the day out of his system. He has a bitter taste in his mouth, spits, and then it rises up from within. He leans over behind a bush and lurches forward, his body tense. He vomits, letting it all spill out of him. It gushes onto the leaves and puddles at his feet. The odor is rank, intense. He continues to throw up until there's nothing but liquid, sour bile from the pit of his stomach, the final dregs leaving his system with a bleating sound. He stands upright once again, wiping around his mouth with his coat sleeve. He sees the ship out in the Oslo fjord. It's almost half past three. His breathing eases. He gathers his thoughts, collecting them like dry leaves, one by one. He had stood there the previous day, just outside their door. He could have knocked. No matter what. He should have knocked.

As Ole Rustad sits in his car, he makes a decision. He starts the engine, the car rolls forward, his thoughts are clear.

S HE SHOULD GET SOME SLEEP. LIE DOWN on the mattress she's sitting on, move Miriam, who has fallen asleep on her lap, close her eyes, disappear. It's nighttime, it must be, Sonja hasn't slept for a whole day and night, she doesn't even feel tired. Miriam lies with her arm wrapped around her doll, there's vomit on the doll's sweater; poor Miriam, her face is so pale, she hadn't managed to say before she had suddenly been sick.

They had been split up upon boarding, women and children toward the rear of the ship, men in the middle. Their father was gone. His face in a crowd, so many others, and then he vanished. The guards shouted. *Los! Los! Schnell!* They ran. They held on tight to their luggage, their mother with the string bag, Sonja with the sack pressing heavily against her back; she felt the tips of a pair of boots she had packed digging into her spine with every step, Miriam's hand in hers, she mustn't lose her grip. Up the steep, slippery ladders, into the narrow corridors of the ship, never fast enough, the guards pushing them, hunting them. A woman stopped to get a better grasp of her suitcase and the guard shoved her to the ground, kicking her; she got up once again, running on without uttering a sound.

They entered a large space where mattresses had been spread over the floor, firm and filthy, filled with wood shavings. No windows, no hatches, guards stationed all around, gloomy lighting. The roaring of the ship. The sounds in the hold, loud voices, yelling, names; many had lost track of their loved ones as they had hurried on board. A boy stood right beside them, a blue jacket and a runny nose; he called out for his mother, a loud, clear sob.

"What's your mother's name?" Sonja asked.

"Mummy," he replied, cross and tearful.

Now Sonja can see that the boy has fallen asleep, he's lying on a mattress a few meters from them while his mother tries to change his little sister. She takes out some fabric from a brown leather case, tears it in two, and wraps it around the lower half of the tiny girl's body, then opens her blouse and holds the baby to her breast.

After a few hours the roaring of the propellers had grown fainter, they had made it out to sea, each person gripping the luggage they had brought with them. The intense stench of vomit mixed with the smell of diesel, wood shavings from the mattresses, sweat, urine, and excrement, so many of them packed into such a small space.

They had eaten the eggs that they had brought with them. Miriam had taken the last, the one intended for Ilse. Her mother hadn't wanted anything. She had become immediately withdrawn after they were separated from their father, sitting and staring all around her, saying nothing. Sonja persuaded her to eat an egg, but she didn't touch the soup they were later offered. She lay on the mattress, whispering until she fell asleep.

Sonja lies down beside Miriam. She puts her arms around her, feels her breathing, calm, the steady rhythm of her heart, the acrid stench of the doll's sweater. It's so quiet in here now. Too quiet. It makes room for so many other sounds. Four days. They were to pack for four days; does that mean they'll be on the ship for four days? And when they get there, where will that be after four days on board, when will they be back, Ilse's dress on the hanger, she sees it, the cotton fabric, the red polka dots, Ilse, the theater job that awaits her, she hasn't given word, the first of December, that's five days from now, she won't be back by then, or will she? She can't close her eyes, can't face it, though she can't face keeping them open either, it's not possible to sleep here, she can't breathe, Miriam's hair tickles her face.

WHAT DAY IS IT NOW? ISAK LIES IN his bunk and thinks. It must be Saturday, the twenty-eighth; they've been traveling for two days now, surely? Days and nights have merged into one; the dim lighting in the cargo hold is the same regardless, nothing to distinguish the hours from one another as they sit or lie down, roll back and forth, yes, it must be Saturday by now.

Quite a few times he's felt himself on the verge of throwing up, the nausea lingering, the hunger, the thirst; he lay down on the hard wooden planks, closed his eyes, and did his very best to disappear. The good old days, the beautiful places, everything that could possibly whisk him away, even for the briefest of split seconds. Image after image flashed by just behind his eyelids.

He lies in bed in his childhood home, the bedsheets clean and white—they smell freshly ironed, and he can hear his mother from the living room, humming softly. The scent of pipe tobacco drifts in through the crack in the doorway, his father's shadow outside the door, his slender silhouette in his armchair. He's nine years old, his parents take good care of him, it's time to go to sleep.

He stands on the bridge by the waterfall, gazing down at the frothing water. It's autumn, a clear October evening, the scent of leaves and fresh earth in the air. Ilse stands by his side, just the two of them, she's throwing autumn leaves over the bridge railing, they drift downward and are swallowed by the volumes of water below them, Ilse smiling; she's missing a tooth.

Image by image, everything is suddenly so close, voices, smells; he can feel the autumn leaves, smell the bedsheets. But then there it is once more: the knowledge of where he is, the uncertainty, where are they going. It won't be possible to escape for a long time yet.

A large room in the center of the ship, bunks three or four beds high, pushed tightly together, endless rows of sleeping spots with no mattresses, no blankets, no pillows—a hard surface to lie on, the wooden planks gnawing away at his body. The old man in the bunk below suffers pain with every move that he makes, limping when he walks. Throughout the first night he had lain and mumbled prayers. Isak couldn't understand him, he must have been speaking Russian, but he had recognized the odd word. In the bunk next to him is a man, he calls out with a groan: "Gerda!" Samuel lies in the bunk above his own. He hasn't said a word for a long while now; it's been a whole day since he last made a single sound.

They hadn't been at sea for more than a few hours before six guards appeared. They patrolled the rows of bunks, pointing all around. *"Du und du und du,"* they screamed, assembling a group of ten or twelve men. One of them was Samuel. The orders flowed.

"Hinlegen!"

The men stood and looked at the guards, quizzical; what did it mean? They learned quickly as they observed others' misfortune. Without warning they swooped in on those who didn't lie down, those who weren't quick enough to follow orders, their rubber clubs raining lightning-fast beatings on shoulders and backs. One order was quickly followed by the next.

"Hüpfen!"

One of the men made a guess and started to hop; the others followed suit. With bent knees and arms out straight in front of them they hopped around. The guards laughed, pointed, found the whole spectacle hilarious, and elsewhere it might have been just that, but not here. One of the guards, a young man with a half-shaven head who was wearing small round spectacles, whispered something to his colleague. Their eyes flashed bright. Quietly they approached the old man in the lower bunk who gazed transfixed at the floor—he panted like an animal, he knew he couldn't escape, he had no chance.

"Now then, old man," the guard with the spectacles said. *"Aufstehen!"*

The old man remained where he was sitting, looking down, his left hand limp and trembling in his lap. The other guard, another young man, gripped him under his arms and hoisted him up, and for a brief moment it looked as if he were helping his grandfather up. The old man looked at him, searching for some sign or other. He didn't need to wait long.

"Rollen!"

The guard with the small spectacles shoved him to the ground, where he lay groaning for a second or two before he was there once again, this time with his steel toe–capped boots. A kick in the stomach, a howl from the floor, and then he followed orders, he and the others who had previously been hopping around. They were to roll on the floor, over and over until there was no breath left in them. The old man tried as hard as he could to do the same as those around him, the younger men, but he wasn't quite fast enough, his efforts weren't quite good enough. He was a cripple, scum, the guards couldn't get enough of his clumsy actions, what entertainment, what a performance.

Now he lies fast asleep in the lower bunk. Isak can hear the rhythm of his breathing. One of his trouser legs has been ripped and his right eye is so swollen that it has closed after its meeting with the guard's boots.

They had to go to the deck of the ship to eat. Up a steep gangway, through the narrow corridors, guards everywhere screaming and shouting at them to hurry. The sea air was damp and cold as it buffeted them with full force after so many hours locked in the cramped cargo hold. They tried to find their bearings, where were they now, where were they headed? The sea swirled black and wild around the ship, engulfed by darkness with the blackout in full effect; even if there were land in sight then they would have no chance of seeing it.

Large soup pans had been placed on a table, but there was nothing to serve the soup in, no bowls, no spoons; the men had to make do with whatever they could find. Many of the older people who hadn't been at Berg had brought utensils and dishes; they'd been told to bring them when they were arrested, one had said, but the prisoners from Berg, the majority of the men, they had nothing with them to speak of. One family had managed to get a washbasin that they filled to the brim with soup and tried to balance as they made their way back to the cargo hold. Isak had nothing. He glanced around the deck, checking to see if there was anything there that he could quickly grab, something he could get his hands on without the guards noticing. There was a guard just beside him. Isak could feel his eyes on him; he had to be careful now, the punishment for taking something, even just rubbish, could be rough.

Then something happened. The guard approached him, looked at him, and for a second they were just two men on a ship, hungry and exhausted after hours spent at sea. He felt something cold against his right hand; there was something there. A tin. The guard nodded swiftly at him and carried on walking.

Isak guzzled the soup from the tin; it was thin, no more than a few potatoes and some pieces of turnip, but even so, it was good. The old man sat by his side and slurped his soup; his wife was on board, he said, she had asthma, did she have enough medication to last the crossing, and what about after that, when they arrived, how would they manage? Would there be a doctor there, could they get more medicine? He needed a walking stick, but they'd already taken it from him at the pier, he said, snapped it in two.

Beside them sat the family with the washbasin. Three of them, the youngest of the lot, had been at Berg, where Isak had noticed that they always stuck together. Now he could hear them whispering around the washbasin. Was it possible to squeeze out of the porthole by the lavatory, could they squeeze through and drop into the sea below, they were all good swimmers after all, but would it work? But what about Ester, one whispered, would they be able to sneak over to the women's quarters and tell her, would she be strong enough? And how cold would the water be at this time of year? Cold, that was for certain, it was late November, how long could a person survive in ice-cold water? Plus, there were guards with machine guns, wouldn't they notice someone in the sea below? They'd be shot at if they didn't drown first. There was a long silence, as if each of them digested the outcome. Then they began to whisper again. Where were they being taken? The oldest of the group, a man with a full beard and a forehead lined with wrinkles, presumably their father, told them about some rumors he'd heard; if it was true that they were going to northern Norway, they'd have to try to find their bearings tomorrow, look out and see if the ship passed Lindesnes and continued north. They weren't yet out of Oslo fjord, their father thought, maybe they'd turn and follow the Norwegian coast northward; there were rumors of a work camp up there. But the women and children, said one son, what good would they be in a work camp? There was silence once again before the men returned to the idea of the porthole: Was it completely impossible?

—

It had taken a long time for them to understand where they were supposed to go when they needed the toilet. Someone had urinated in a corner of the cargo hold, squeezing in as close as possible to the wall, letting it flow from them. But after a few hours at sea, someone had approached one of the guards. He held his hands in front of his lower abdomen, made a trickling sound, a long "ssshh," and asked "*Warum?*" possibly the only question word he knew in German. The guard had thumped him with a clenched fist that had flown fast, clipping the man around the ear. An older man in a black suit approached the same guard.

"*Bitte austreten zu dürfen?*"

The guard looked at the man, who stood with his head bowed, staring at the ground. Something stirred on his lips, a sneer, a scornful snicker; would the man receive the same treatment, would there be more beatings to come? After a moment the guard pointed up toward the deck and explained in German where they should go. The porthole set into the hull of the ship, it could be opened, Isak had seen it. But to slip out, drop into the sea? Hanna and Sonja and Miriam, he couldn't abandon them, and he wasn't a particularly good swimmer.

Now he lies in his bunk, above the old man and below Samuel, his eyes closed. He's sitting in his armchair at home; he can smell coffee, freshly brewed, the sun glitters through the apartment windows, is the wireless on? He can hear something. A voice. Someone singing. A woman. He opens his eyes. He lowers his head and leans out of his bunk, sees those sitting and lying all around, the prisoners, it doesn't look as if they can believe what they're hearing. *I was only eighteen when you first met me, the moon laughed and we danced to the most elegant melody.* That song, he knows it so well, usually whistles along, but now he keeps his lips firmly sealed. He leans back in his bunk. It's coming now, he can feel it, he can't remember the last time, it rises upward, slow, deep twitches moving through him. He presses his face against the hard wooden planks and feels the tears sting his eyes.

Sonja awakens with a jolt. It's the train, it's stopped again, she has no idea for how long she has been sleeping. She can hear the sound of voices outside the carriage, someone calling out, messages, the brief exchange of words. Light from the floodlights outside seeps in through the peepholes in the wall. It illuminates the upper half of the carriage, falling on the faces of those still standing. They're huddled close, entangled, bolt upright like matchsticks packed into a tiny matchbox. Miriam has curled up in a ball on the floor, up against the wall with her hat pulled down over her ears and her legs tucked underneath her. Sonja can feel the weight of her body against her feet. The lurch of the train hasn't woken her. Her mother stands by her side, and though her eyes are closed Sonja knows that she isn't sleeping. Occasionally she opens her eyes slightly, just enough that she can see and no more, glancing around her and then tightly squeezing them closed once again. She's been standing this way,

215

eyes firmly shut, ever since they'd managed to calm her down.

Someone cries out for water. They've asked for the same thing every time that the train has come to a standstill, *Wasser, bitte, Wasser,* a chorus of hoarse voices from dry, cavernous mouths. They haven't been given any water for several hours, not since they were back on board the ship. Sonja can hear the sound of her own voice in her mind, *Wasser, Wasser,* she can't tell whether she's saying the words aloud or simply churning over them in her own head; her lips sting, there's no trace of moisture in her mouth.

She hears a carriage being connected to or perhaps even disconnected from their own and the train lurches forward yet again, the movement causing her to jostle Miriam. It happens every time that the train stops. The brakes screech, then they hear the sound of footsteps outside, trains whooshing past them, a shrill whistle, a lurching carriage, then the journey continues once more.

Now they're on the move once again, they sway from side to side; the rhythm of the train has worked its way into her system, a few jerks to the left, a few more to the right, back and forth. Darkness has fallen; it must be late afternoon. All day and night they have stood here. Through a crack in the wooden planks she has managed to catch the faintest glimpses of the landscape outside. Trees blanketed in snow, the odd village, gray railway stations, unknown place names on signs.

The woman behind her gasps for air again, another fit. Her chest wheezes, her voice gurgles.

"I can't breathe," she cries. "Help me, please."

Her head falls back and she opens her mouth, greedily gulping at the cold air in the carriage before coughing it back up again. She's asthmatic, she had told Sonja, she had no medication with her; I'll suffocate, she cried several times. Her breath smells rotten, a mixture of dried blood and spoiled food, intense and pressing; it mixes with the strong stench of urine. Sonja is aware that the woman has wet herself, they are pressed together so tightly that she can feel her damp clothing. Her husband is in a different carriage, she said, she can't imagine how he'll manage to stand all this time, perhaps he's managed to find somewhere to sit down. She whispers prayers in a language Sonja can't understand, it sounds like Russian, a multitude of words in a steady stream of dry murmurs.

Sonja can't pray any longer. She's tried closing her eyes, gathering her thoughts and finding the words, but now, now there are only fragments, oh God, oh God, oh God, nothing more.

After they'd spent four days in the cargo hold, the ship had reached the quay. The waves eased, the rhythm changed, the doors were opened, and the passengers, exhausted after the long journey, were ordered to make their way up onto the ship's deck. Sonja held Miriam's hand, their mother behind them hauling the sack. They walked from the warm, overcrowded cargo hold into the biting cold. It was freezing outside, the air stinging their lungs as they inhaled, the insides of their noses numbed by the air they drew in. Huge wooden planks had been propped up against the side of the ship; Sonja watched as many of the men slipped on them on their way down onto land. Women and children were permitted to use the same ladders they'd been instructed to use to climb on board. The ice made every rung slippery, and everything had to be done quickly. There were the same barks, calls, and shoves, and laughter every time that anyone slipped.

The quayside had been teeming with guards. Men were sent to the left while women and children were instructed to go right. Sonja had looked for her father, gazing into the throng of men that swarmed to her left, but she couldn't see him, there were so many people there. Miriam called out for him; many others did the same thing. Her mother stood in perfect silence. It looked as if they'd arrived in a town, concrete port facilities, enormous steel cranes dangling over the pier, bright floodlights casting a garish glare, snow falling lightly. A railway track disappeared into the distant white landscape.

They were herded in the direction of the train track where a train stood ready, carriage doors open, gaping before them like dark voids; they ran with their luggage in hand. They were sorted alphabetically. Men in one part of the train, women and children in another. The first carriage was filled, the doors shoved closed with hard, heavy thuds, people crying out from inside, Sonja could hear it all. They were directed to one of the last carriages, up against the farthest wall; they could feel the weight of a steady stream of passengers being pushed into the carriage. It was so tightly packed that they had to remain standing, shoulder to shoulder, then someone lost their footing, fell down onto the ground and was trodden on by one of the others. The doors were closed, for a moment there was utter darkness, the only light in the carriage coming from the peepholes high up on the wall. Sonja lifted Miriam, held her close, leaned against the wall. The long blast of a whistle was followed by the first trundling lurches of the carriage, and then the train began to move.

At one point everyone had been standing upright, but as the hours crept by people had tried to move around, creating small spaces by their feet where some could crouch down. Miriam was against the wall, the cold air seeping in through the gaps in the planks of wood. Sonja had taken a blanket from the sack containing their belongings and had laid it over Miriam; she had done what she could to tuck her in, to prevent her from getting too cold.

It was quiet in the train carriage. Close together, bodies in contact, the rhythmic sound of the train was all that could be heard. *Gadong gadong. Gadong gadong.* Sonja rested her head against the wall, felt the way it drummed against the planks of wood, closed her eyes and opened them again. Through the gaps she could see expanses of white outside, everything blanketed in snow. They passed a farm, children playing outside.

After a few hours on board their mother had started to hammer at the walls. First gently, a silent, steady thudding. Her hand crept over the planks as if seeking a hidden opening, a loose plank that might allow them the chance to hop out into the snow. But then suddenly it was as if something flared up within her, blazing bright, an imprisoned cry. She began to shove those around her with reckless abandon, barging into the old Russian lady, stepping on a woman in a fur coat who lay on the floor, her arms waving around in the air. Sonja tried putting her arms around her, holding her tight, but her mother broke free, elbowing her way through the group of tightly packed bodies; she needed out, she hissed.

Now she's standing with her eyes squeezed tightly shut. Her body moves in time with the train's rhythm; she's calm now, unreachable. The wound over her eye has dried to form an oval scab, her eyelids look so delicate and fine, transparent. She looks like an old woman, confused and ashamed after having allowed herself to openly panic in such a way, calm like a small child soothed to sleep after a tantrum.

What day is it now? It must be Tuesday. Only a week since they had eaten herring for dinner; it had been sour and rancid, but even so, they had been gathered around the table on Biermanns gate. Ilse had told her about Hermann that evening; they'd been whispering together as they lay in bed. Sonja had come so close to telling Ilse of her plans, but she couldn't find the words, she had let Ilse do most of the talking. It seemed like an eternity since that moment.

Tuesday? She should be somewhere else now. Ascending the carpeted staircase, enveloped by the pleasant scents of the theater, sitting behind a sewing machine, the winter sunshine through the oval windows lighting up her face. She should have been greeting the other seamstresses, signing papers in Mr. Østli's office.

Today is the first of December. Tuesday. She should be somewhere else.

The train slows. The brakes screech as it comes to a complete standstill. Miriam stands up. They hear voices outside, voices and something else—animals, dogs, barking impatiently. Nobody asks for water. Everyone stands in silence. It is as if they know. They have arrived. Sonja hears the bolts being lifted. The sound of steel, heavy and hard. A white light from the large floodlights streams into the carriage. Men swarm outside, packs of dogs rearing at their leashes. The icy haze forms a cloud around their muzzles. The passengers walk toward the white light, toward the open door, tumbling out of the carriages, their bodies stiff after a day and night, perhaps longer, spent almost stationary. Sonja catches sight of a sign hanging over the platform: *Auschwitz*. It means nothing to her.

T HINGS MOVE QUICKLY. THEY'RE FORCED
out of the carriages and hop down onto the
platform. There are no ladders or boards to
help them down and several people stumble as they
attempt to clamber out. Sonja sees the old Russian
woman; she lands on the ground like a heavy sack, then
totters back onto her feet, gasping for air with regular
wheezes. There are so many people here, the guards call
out, the same cries they've heard for the past few days,
always the same; they need to hurry, they're nothing
but a pack of swine, run, come on, run.

"*Männer links. Frauen und Kinder rechts.*" The
loudspeaker booms, crackles.

Sonja, her mother, and Miriam run over to the
right with the other women and children; they flock
together.

Large trucks drive in, tarpaulins over the flatbeds, the
loudspeaker crackling once again. They are instructed
to leave all of their bags in a pile. Several hesitate,

unwilling to leave all that they own, all that they've brought with them from home. The bags will be forwarded on to them afterward, they're told, they should leave them, everyone will have their belongings returned to them in due course. Sonja takes the string bag and the coarse woolen sack. She adds them to the growing pile of suitcases and bags.

They hurry over, the prisoners in striped coveralls, so frail and pale that they look as if they've forgotten to perish. The prison uniforms hang from their skinny frames; it looks as if they might snap in two at any moment. Only their eyes are alive, large and dark; they move quickly in their slim faces, darting from person to person. They quickly haul every item of baggage up onto the flatbeds of the trucks. A few trucks drive away.

A new order is roared. Women, children, and elderly men are to board the trucks that remain. The flock is driven toward the vehicles. They run. The air is filled with cries and screams and barks. Sonja lifts Miriam up onto the back of the truck before climbing up beside her and turning to offer her mother a hand. They keep close to one another beneath the tarpaulin, standing tall, shoulder to shoulder. Before the back of the truck is slammed shut, Sonja catches sight of her father. Lined up with the other men in a row, he looks in their direction, one man within a teeming crowd of hundreds. She calls out to him, waves her arms, but he doesn't see her; the truck doors are slammed shut, the engine starts, and the truck begins to drive away.

Through a gap in the tarpaulin Sonja can see low brick buildings, long rows of dark blocks in the grayish light. Evening sets in, dark and chilly, the air like tiny arrows striking her lungs. There's something here, a smell, it reminds her of the stench of the rubbish in the passageway at home.

The truck comes to a halt. They park in front of two barracks. A tall man greets them. Behind him are prisoners, the same uniforms, the same large eyes, the same stooped posture.

"*Ich brauche einen Dolmetscher,*" the man says, looking around him.

His voice carries a different tone, not strict, not sharp, but friendly. An elderly man raises a hand. He's plucked out of the crowd to stand by the man's side and translate.

"You are now standing at the entrance to a camp. In this camp there are strict rules relating to hygiene. You have undertaken a long and arduous journey, and you must now bathe. Remove your clothing in the changing room and hang this on the pegs provided. Make sure to remember your peg number—this will make it easier to find your clothing again later. In this camp, men and women share bathing facilities. Women and children will enter first, men afterward. Wash thoroughly and exit through the door marked 'Zur Desinfektion.' You will then be provided with a towel. Understand?"

Nobody answers; nobody says a word.

They walk into the changing room, take off their clothes, and hang them from the pegs. Two nine seven three. Sonja makes a mental note of the number. They continue into an oblong room. The walls have been painted white, with a row of showerheads protruding from them. There is a strange smell within the room, intense and strong, not necessarily bad, just strange. Sonja hugs Miriam close, her bare body thin, her small arms wrapped around Sonja's waist. She hugs her mother, her breathing labored, her cold skin carrying the smell of sweat. She sees Erik, his mother's hand cupping his cheek, her bulging stomach, her navel like a button protruding from her abdomen. The old Russian lady holds her hands in front of her face, her skin hanging in folds from her strong frame; she coughs.

The doors close again with a bang. The room falls into darkness. They wait for the water. Long, drawn-out seconds. Several of them call out. Loud screams. Sonja stands silent. Her mouth is closed. Miriam's head rests against her stomach. Her hair is soft. It is still dark. Pitch-black. Impossible to breathe.

ISAK HOLDS HIS BREATH, PAUSING WITH the air in his lungs for as long as he is able to, as if to warm himself with his own breath, store it in his body to get through the night. They lie there naked, most curled up in the fetal position, their legs folded beneath them as if to make themselves as small as possible, poised to best defend themselves. They are in a bathroom; it must be below freezing in here.

He had looked for them when the trucks had arrived. Women, children, old people, all up onto the flatbed of the trucks, it had happened so quickly, there were so many of them, he hadn't managed to catch sight of them.

The trucks had driven off and the men left behind were ordered to form rows of five. The commands rang out in the darkness of the night.

"Vordermann! Abstand nehmen! Im Gleichschritt marsch!"

They were headed for the unknown. The mud underfoot had frozen, now forming hard sheets; the air was rank, a peculiar smell all around. They marched through a large set of double gates, barbed wire above and below them, the light from the large floodlights in two towers swiping over them, swiping over the area, the brief flashes of light making it possible to form an idea of where they might have arrived. Inside the gate Isak could see long rows of gray brick barracks, an entire landscape of low buildings. Between the buildings emerged a few figures in striped uniforms. The prisoners shuffled as if they couldn't face the prospect of lifting their feet from the ground beneath them, as if they lacked the strength required to move just a few meters. Isak stared at them. How long could they have been here? It didn't look as if they had ever lived an ordinary life. Would he be here long enough to become that way too, nothing but skin and bone, shuffling along in a striped suit?

They continued through more double gateways and over into another camp, Birkenau. Large concrete structures with tall, quadrangular chimney stacks. There, just beyond the fence, there were hundreds of striped uniforms, the place was crawling with them. And just beyond that, in the dark doorway of the concrete buildings, stark naked people. They were being chased. Don't look, one person said, someone in his own row, and Isak had looked down, concentrated on his own two feet, his shoes, the mud.

The line of men stopped. They were ordered into one of the barracks. There were bunks on three levels, tightly packed rows lining the walls, eight men to each bunk, all sharing a blanket. They hadn't been lying down for many minutes before a guard was there, his voice tearing through the darkness, his cries ringing out in the space.

"*Aufstehen!*"

They hopped out of their bunks and onto the floor; hadn't they just been told to go to sleep? And now this, what next, which rules were they supposed to obey?

A man dressed in a black uniform and polished riding boots stood at the end of the room, flanked by a small group of men in prison coveralls that looked different from the others they'd seen outside; muscle-bound men standing in a semicircle. The man in uniform moved farther into the room, closer, heavy footsteps, his boots squeaking as he paced the floor. Samuel stood beside Isak. He trembled; he wasn't able to control the shaking throughout his body. The guard in riding boots neared the pair, walking right up to them and stopping in front of Samuel.

"*Was bist du von Beruf, du Judenschwein?*"

His voice was soft, almost animated. Samuel said nothing. The guard breathed heavily; Isak could feel it, strong, alcohol.

"Du bist ein Geschäftsmann, was?"

Samuel shook his head slowly; no, he wasn't a shop-keeper. It looked as if he was trying to think of a word; he didn't know much German. The guard hawked up a globule of phlegm and spat it in the direction of Samuel's face. He carried on walking, asking others the same question. If they couldn't muster a response, he spat at them. If they could, he hit them. He beat them in the manner of a short-tempered young boy, aiming where he knew he would cause the most pain.

After a while he signaled to one of the others, a short, stocky man with a green patch on his chest.

"As you know, you have been brought here, to this labor camp," he said, thrusting his arms out as if he'd been instructed to give them a warm welcome.

"Here you will be tasked with similar employment to that which you held previously. Those who work with diligence will be rewarded with an appropriate salary. In a month or two you may visit your family and friends."

He paused. There was something concealed in his gaze, as if all of this were somehow rehearsed, his eyes flitting here and there along the rows of men.

"Questions?"

For a moment they all stood in silence. Nobody dared say a word. The man with the green patch on the chest of his coveralls waited. A prisoner ventured a hand in the air.

"Yes?"

In clumsy German, the prisoner inquired about how they might make contact with their families. The man with the green patch smiled at him, nodding slowly, as if he had asked a good question, as if he were carefully considering his response.

"Just come to me," he said after a long pause, laughter flashing in his eyes. "Come to me and you can borrow my bicycle."

The guards laughed. The man with the green patch wandered over to them, accepting his applause and jovial slaps on the shoulder, running his hand through his hair.

They turned back to their bunks, attempting to lie in some kind of formation, four with their heads at one end and four with their heads at the other, their legs weaved together. They shared the only blanket they had, draping it over their legs. Isak lay on the outside. He thought about the others, wondered if things were any better in the women's quarters; was it equally crowded in there, did they have better bunks, more blankets? The naked people they'd caught a glimpse of in the doorway. Most of them had been women. It had been only a few seconds, but it had seemed just as crowded, he'd seen it with his own eyes, it had been just long enough to catch a proper glimpse; he would never forget such a sight. Some of the men had been convinced it wasn't real, just some kind of trick of the eye using film that was designed to break them down.

How long could he survive here? Was it even possible? What about the others? And Ilse. He lay for a long while, thinking, on edge. A single lightbulb emitted a dull glow above a bucket intended for relieving themselves in at the end of the room.

He couldn't have been asleep for long before he became aware of it: cold fingers creeping along the edge of the bunk, back and forth, as if looking for something. When he opened his eyes, he was staring directly into a man's face. Two large eyes gazed back at him, a pair of enormous ears sticking out from a smoothly shaven head beneath a striped cap, his cheeks so hollow that it looked as if he had spooned out the flesh and stretched the remaining skin over the open wound. There was a yellow star on his coveralls. The man quickly withdrew his hand and stood by the bunk, completely still as if waiting for something to happen.

"*Parlez-vous français?*" he whispered.

Isak shook his head.

"*Jiddisch?*"

"*Nein. Deutsch?*"

Isak's German wasn't particularly good, but he could understand a fair amount. The figure moved with strange, stiff gestures, like a wooden marionette puppet, a few steps forward, then a few back, and then there he was once again. He held Isak's gaze, his focus entirely fixed as if he was suddenly concentrating. He whispered for a long time, word after word tumbling from his toothless mouth. Isak listened.

At daybreak they were woken by a roar.

"*Aufstehen!*"

They rose to their feet and lined up alongside the rows of bunks. Metal containers filled with brown liquid were passed around, a kind of tea, everyone forced to drink from the same container. For a moment Isak wondered if he should pass, the prisoner's advice in the back of his mind. The mixing of saliva, all kinds of bacteria. But as soon as the container reached his hands, his thirst took over and he gulped at the contents.

Up in lines, they marched out of the barracks and across a square, the snow falling heavily. They stopped outside a white building and were directed into an oblong room with wooden benches lining both sides. Their clothing was to be folded neatly and placed on the bench. The floor was ice cold beneath their bare feet; it gave them goose bumps. Several of them placed their hands in front of their genitals, trying to protect themselves, to shield their naked white bodies. On the wall were two large signs, fat black lettering above a skull with an X through it: *Ein Laus — dein Tod.*

In the next room were more prisoners seated behind low tables, electric razors and scissors laid out at the ready. The hair on their heads. Isak bowed his head and watched as it fell to the floor in thick tufts, his dark brown locks mixing with the hair of the others that had been standing in front of him in the line, the electric razors buzzing. The hair on their bodies. It was simply a case of standing still and allowing the prisoners to carry out their assigned task. Naked and hairless, they were driven farther into a bathroom with showerheads that protruded from the walls. The showers were switched on and ice-cold water gushed forth; his skin stung, the stream of water hitting his upper body like spearheads. The water stopped for a moment and was then turned on once again, this time so hot that he was scalded. The room began to fill with steam, rising from the floor. Hot water, cold water, hot, cold, how long would this go on, how long had they already stood there, hunched over with their arms wrapped around them?

The tattooists were short of time. They were heavy-handed with their equipment, the numbers appearing crooked and knotted on his skin, his left forearm, a number that was now his new name, his new identity.

They were assigned a card. On the left side information about each of them had been added to the blank sections. Isak stood with his card in his hand. So there he was, Isak Stern: forty years old, no gold teeth, naked and shaven, one man in a crowd of many others, some numbers on his forearm and a few words written on a single slip of paper. On the right were just three words: *Date of Death.* It had been left blank.

He lies there in the freezing-cold bathroom where they're to spend the night. Isak exhales slowly through his mouth in short wheezes. He draws air in deep through his nostrils, holding it for as long as he can in his lungs before letting it filter out between his lips. He can feel his smooth head against his forearm, sense the questions that linger and quiver within him, uncertainty, nausea. The toothless mouth, the prisoner from yesterday, his words, he must remember them. Never let them see that you're sick. Pretend that you're in good health. Never answer yes. Never no. Only answer when there's no chance at all of getting away without doing so. Never run, even if you're ordered to. If you run, they'll shoot you for attempting escape. Forget where you come from, forget who you are, forget that you were once human.

He has to use his instincts now. Work with his intuition. Sniff out the way forward. Hunt. He has to become an animal.

AYS. SIX HAVE PASSED SO FAR. ILSE has remained inside the red room. She has sat on the edge of the bed or curled up under the duvet and stared up at the ceiling. Occasionally Einar Vindju has opened the door and looked in on her. He never says much, just brings her something to eat, placing a plate on the bedside table and closing the door behind him. The rest of the time she has been left to her own devices. The four red walls, the coving on the ceiling, she knows the pattern inside out, the silence of the room allows for so much other noise to intrude, so many thoughts. Mum. Miriam. Sonja. She can hear their voices, their breathing, the wrinkles around her mother's mouth, she can picture them so clearly, she'd told her that she hated her, had screamed it in her face before leaving, she can't, it's impossible, can't think about that now. She closes her eyes, lies on the bed, and there they are, at home, the whole family. The crowded apartment, the living room, the windows, the sounds of the street outside, the smell of food, her mother's cooking.

On the first morning Einar had come in to see her, telling her that he'd be gone for a few hours.

"Keep away from the window," he had said, placing a tea plate with two slices of bread on the bedside table. "Nobody can know that you're here, you see." He smiled. Drew a match, lit a cigarette, blew smoke rings inside the room.

It was so silent after he left. No sound from the neighbors, no commotion from the stairwell, no crying or shouting children. It was so different from what she was used to. As if she were all alone in the huge tenement building, as if there weren't a single other person on any of the other floors. She lay in her bed, her body aching. After a few hours she got up. She should be quiet, Einar had told her, but without thinking too much about it her legs began to move. She stalked her way around, first in the red room, from the bed and over to the wardrobe against the wall, opening the doors and peering inside: empty shelves, a few clothing hangers on a rail. She closed the wardrobe door. She opened the door that led into the hallway, darkness, doors, so many doors, all closed; she walked toward the entrance. The glass door into the parlor, she coaxed the sliding door open carefully, pushing it to one side and staring into the large room. There were painting things everywhere, it looked more like a studio than a room in a house, the scent of chemicals tearing at the inside of her nostrils. On an easel by the window stood a half-finished painting: a plump, naked body in shades of blue. She ran a hand over the picture, felt the way the paint had been applied in thick layers in certain sections. The sunlight beamed through the large window and spread throughout the room, the sky outside a bright shade of blue. In a few hours it would be dark.

She walked back along the hallway. How many rooms could there be here? Eight doors. Did he have eight rooms?

There had been others here before her, he'd said, as if it were some kind of hotel that he was running. Who were they? Young girls like her? Others all on their own? Other Jews?

Hermann Rød. He still hasn't come. She had waited for him on the first day, on all the other days after that too, waited and hoped that he would appear, but it has been quiet. She wonders why he hasn't been, why he's dropped her off here and left, sent no word; he had said he'd be back. She asked Einar about it, if he'd heard from Hermann; he didn't reply, instead simply shrugging his shoulders and hurrying out of the room.

On the first day Einar had been gone all day long. Now he's back again, in the apartment, all the time. He sits in the kitchen. Smokes. He never opens the front door when anyone knocks.

She lies on the bed with her nose buried in Hermann's sweater; it still smells like him, soft and boyish.

The door into the hallway is open and suddenly she hears a voice, Einar, he's on the telephone in the kitchen. She tries to make out what he's saying, he speaks in hushed tones; the only word she can make out is "turnip." Turnip? Was he running some kind of black market operation? She closes the door, once again returning to the bed.

"Ilse," Einar says from the doorway, walking over and sitting beside her on the edge of the bed. "I need you to listen carefully. In one hour you must go out onto the street. You will walk to Frognerveien and stand in front of the grocery shop. Stay there and look in the window until a man approaches you and introduces himself as Andersen. He'll ask you if you are Inger, and you will say yes. The man will take you somewhere else."

He takes a deep breath.

"Do you understand everything I've told you?"

"Yes," Ilse whispers, looking at him. "I understand."

Outside it has started to grow dark. The streets are wide open and empty, the sidewalks shining in the light drizzle. She crosses the street and the tenement building looms behind her. She can see Einar at the living room window, no more than a vague shape, a gray body up there above her. The rain falls softly on her forehead; she keeps her eyes to the ground as she walks. She doesn't know the area well; the names on the street signs still seem foreign to her. Einar has given her clear directions, his words linger in her mind; according to what he had told her she should almost be there, but what if she were to make a mistake? What if she hadn't been listening properly?

Frognerveien, she spots the road sign. She needs to take a left here and follow the road upward. The shop is on the left side of the street, she searches for it in the gloomy, dwindling light. Twenty meters farther she spots a white sign hanging over a doorway.

She stands in front of the shop window and peers at the meager selection of goods advertised. *Fish skin shoes. Cowberries from Voksenkollen. Do you have old sheets at home? They can be transformed into children's clothing.* The shop. Her father. Suddenly she pictures him behind the cash desk, the scent of brown paper, the sound of Sonja behind the sewing machine.

A man in a brown coat crosses the street. She stands still, hearing the way his galoshes slap against the asphalt, noting every step as he approaches her; he's right behind her now. He stops there; she can hear the sound of his breathing, the scent of tobacco.

"Now then, miss, are you standing here and dreaming of better times?"

She doesn't turn around. She stands motionless, as if she were a doll on display in the window, an extension of the darkened grocery shop.

"May I offer you a cigarette, miss?"

She doesn't move an inch. Wishes that he would go. She can't stand here and make small talk, not now.

"Do you live around here, miss?"

He could be Andersen. Maybe he just wants her to turn around so he can ask her if she's Inger, maybe all he wants is eye contact with her, just so he can explain who he is?

She turns her head slightly, looking at him. A young man; he smiles at her.

"Where are you off to, miss?"

What should she say? She stands there with her mouth half open and gazes at him, waiting for him to utter the magic word: Andersen. He stands there. Still smiling. But he doesn't say it.

"Now then, what do you say, miss? Would you like a cigarette?"

At that moment she catches sight of something else. A shadow, something dark, on the opposite side of the street, half concealed behind a tree.

"No, thank you," she says, giving a cautious smile. "I need to go home now."

She turns around and walks in the opposite direction, crossing the street. Just as long as he doesn't follow her, as long as he continues on his way. She listens for the sound of his galoshes, stops for a moment to hear more clearly. Yes, there's someone walking behind her. She turns to see whether it's the young man. It's not him. It is the man she had just seen standing by the tree. She stands still; she can hear him getting closer; she doesn't turn around before she hears his voice.

"Inger?" he whispers.

She nods. He takes her arm in his own, as if they were father and daughter, out together in the evening drizzle, making their way home. He doesn't say another word, simply walks and stares into the distance. It is as if he has no face, no voice, only a body that guides her through the wet city streets. They turn onto Kirkeveien, Frogner Park just across the road from them, dark and quiet like a gaping black hole. They pass by Kirkeveien 23, the same building, it's quiet there now, a few guards out smoking under the shelter of a small roof.

Farther up the street they turn right. Middelthuns gate, he stops outside a brown door, rings one of the bells, *Wesnes* written beside it. Behind the frosted glass of the front door Ilse sees a shadow approaching, closer and closer. The door opens, revealing a woman wearing a white apron, her fair hair pinned up neatly. She sticks her head out.

"How lovely to see you!" she loudly announces in a Bergen dialect, glancing momentarily around them in the street. "Come in."

Once inside, everything unfolds as if in a silent film, facts exchanged swiftly, as if Andersen were delivering a package, something changing hands, traded goods.

"Very well," the woman whispers, giving Andersen a sign and pointing behind her. He creeps down a set of stairs, opens a door, and disappears out into what looks to be a backyard.

"You come with me," the woman says to Ilse, her tone gentle, caring. "My name is Ellen." She takes Ilse's hand and leads her up to the next floor.

Two broad doors lead into the apartments upstairs. She opens the door to the left and lets Ilse in first.

THE ROOM IS SMALL AND CRAMPED, square, the air stale, cool and raw. If he stands against one wall, he can walk exactly four steps before having to turn back around. Hermann does exactly this. He walks four steps, stops, and turns around. High up on one wall is a narrow opening, a tiny window. It is closed, and in front of the glass are bars, closely spaced; it would be impossible to slip a hand through. If he stands directly underneath the window, he can take exactly four steps before he bumps into the door. He starts pacing, one, two, three, four, lays his hand against the cold steel door, turns and walks in the opposite direction, one, two, then stops. He stands in the middle of the room, his arms by his side, feels their weight, the way they hang by his body, the faint prickling sensation within them. He feels the numbness, the anxiety. They could be back any minute. He mustn't talk.

—

Ilse. She had been sitting on the bed when he left. He is still wearing the same clothes now, he was supposed to go back, he had promised her, she's waiting for him—Einar, he hasn't managed to get word to him.

He had walked all the way home after taking Ilse to Frogner that day. There was nobody outside the building, nobody in the backyard, he let himself in and started making his way up the stairs, a light jog, taking several steps at a time. Just as he was about to reach his front door on the third floor, he heard a sound, a voice. He turned around. Ole Rustad stood on the landing between the third and fourth floors, leaning over the railing and waving his arms, whispering something, fast and impossible to fathom.

The door to the apartment opened. Ole Rustad vanished.

"Hermann Rød?" The voice was high-pitched; he recognized it.

The policeman shoved him inside the apartment.

His mother and father stood beside each other in the living room, clothes and blankets all over the floor, furniture in all the wrong places. The policeman with the high-pitched voice and a man in a gray coat and heavy boots stood in the middle of the room.

"We're looking for Ilse Stern," the policeman said. "We strongly suspect that you have something to do with her disappearance."

Silence. The policeman coughed.

His mother was in her apron, she avoided his gaze; his father was in his undershirt, his arms crossed over his chest.

"I've told them, Hermann, that you've been with that painter in Frogner, that you take evening classes, that you were there all day yesterday."

His father walked over to the sofa, leaned over, and pulled out one of the paintings. His alibi. He hadn't ever expected it to be a credible one, he couldn't even draw a straight line, yet there stood his father, holding the picture, showing it off, just as Hermann had done himself all those times he'd come home to his parents.

"What's his name again, Hermann? Tell them, Hermann, what's his name?"

Møllergata 19. They'd driven him there, escorted him out of the backseat and into the building, down into the cellar, along the narrow corridors, down into the darkness, into a cell, closed the door. He'd come up with a name, a different address. But Frogner, how many artists lived there, how long would it take the police to form a list, look them up? They'd already been at Einar's door, on the same day that he was supposed to meet

Ilse to go to the pictures. He imagines Einar's apartment, someone breaking into the yellow room, tearing away the thick blankets that blacked out the windows, daylight breaking through and illuminating everything inside the room: the typewriter, the wireless in the dark brown box, the piles of paper, Ilse in the neighboring room, the whole universe they'd established there—he pictures it all, exposed.

Now he lies on a bench and stares up at a point on the ceiling. There's a crack up above him, a long line that inches toward the center of the room. For a moment it is as if he is lying in his own bed in the living room at home, lying there and staring at the ceiling before finally drifting off to sleep, so many nights spent the same way, motionless, tense, just staring upward.

Nobody has spoken to him for several days. He suspects this is part of the game they're playing with him, breaking him down, eradicating any trace of resistance—then all that remains is to launch their attack, gorge themselves, extract the confessions from him one by one. He recalls the day he had met with Einar and heard that they'd brought in the death penalty. Would they implement it now; was all of this worth dying for?

Einar would no doubt say yes, but what about him? He twists and turns, his pulse rate increasing, his head thumping. He has to keep quiet. Just a few more days, so Ilse can get away. Einar must know that something has happened, but just a few more days, he has to keep his mouth shut.

He drifts in and out of light sleep, escaping into a dream before being roused by the sound of footsteps in the corridor, keys. He stands up and stares at the door. He watches as it opens, hears the creak of the hinges. They've come to fetch him. He holds his breath. Tenses his muscles until they burn. Seals his lips.

D AYS AND NIGHTS. DAYS AND NIGHTS. How many have passed? Time is erased, the hours merging into one another like sticky shadows, filled with minutes and seconds, thoughts back and forth. Unease. Ilse has been sleeping in a small maid's room just off the kitchen. A narrow bed pushed up against one wall, a bedside table, a window facing the backyard, a mirror over a chest of drawers.

"Do you like reading?" Ellen had asked her on one of her first days there.

She had brought her a book that had been left there by her daughter, who had married a few years ago and since moved out; it was curling at the corners and smelled dusty, a romance novel. Ilse had allowed her eyes to rest on the pages of the book, reading the same words over and over again. When she reached the final page, she closed the book and couldn't recall a single word of what she had just read.

She can hear Ellen in the kitchen clattering pots and pans, the sound of running water, glasses and plates clinking against the bottom of the sink. So similar, these sounds. It could have been any old kitchen. Her mother, leaning over the sink, drying the wet dishes with a blue-checked tea towel, stacking them on the shelves above the kitchen table.

Ellen brought her meals. On the first day she had asked Ilse if she wanted to join her and her husband in the kitchen. The prospect of sitting at the table for a whole meal was too much, she couldn't face it, she was so tired, lifeless. Ellen placed a plate on her bedside table, patted her lightly on the head, and closed the door behind her as she left the room. Ilse had taken one bite and had promptly fallen asleep. When she woke again several hours later, the food was still there, a few cold potatoes and a rubbery piece of fish.

Days and nights. It must have been over a week now. Just how long will she be here for?

One evening she stood in front of the mirror. It was old and distorted, and everything looked crooked in the wobbly glass; her cheekbones rippled, Hermann's sweater draped over her body like a loose curtain. Was this Ilse Stern? A skinny, empty body, indistinct features staring back at her. She thought about all of the effort she had gone to, all of her attempts to improve her appearance, Vaseline on her eyelids, a warm cloth over her face twice each day, the two balls of yarn she'd placed inside her tight-fitting, childish undershirt. And now?

Ellen had come in one evening and had sat on the edge of her bed. She gave Ilse a tender look, said nothing, just sat there with her hands in her lap. She breathed slowly and softly. She looked to be in her fifties, maybe even sixties. She had deep wrinkles around her eyes, a slight double chin, her hair pinned up as if she were going to a party.

"We're doing our best to arrange transportation," she said. "It shouldn't have taken as long as this, but we're doing all that we can, just so you know."

She stood up and patted Ilse gently on the head. Go, Ilse thought, just go, close the door, get out, go now. First it was just a slight gasp, a faint exhale, but then, with Ellen's hand still resting on her head, Ilse could feel it opening up within her, burning upward and through her.

"It'll be all right," Ellen whispered. "It'll be all right, my girl."

How could she say that? It was impossible to think that anything would ever be all right again, that she would ever smile or laugh; it couldn't be. Days and nights, that's what it was, everything that had passed and everything that was yet to come, just days and nights, everything, her, alone.

She woke in the morning to find Ellen by her bed once again. Her eyes were narrow, her hair pinned up in a tight bun.

"I need you to listen very carefully," she said, sitting close to Ilse.

Ilse walks along the street. It's snowed since she was last outside, it's wet; the snow creaks as she steps in it. She's almost there. There, at the crossroad, that's where she's been told she should stop and wait. A black taxi, Ellen had said, it'll be parked over by the large oak tree on Jacob Aalls gate. The engine will be off and the driver will be sitting and reading a book. She should open the back door and sit inside. She shouldn't say anything about who she is or where she's going.

On the other side of the street by the bank of snow and the tree sits a black car. Ilse looks one way and then the other along the street, crosses at the pedestrian crossing, and walks up alongside the taxi.

H E READS THE SAME SENTENCES OVER and over again as he waits, as if the words are the only things he has to cling on to, a string of letters suspended over a deep canyon he mustn't tumble into. He has opened the book at a random page in the middle, words, so many words, he balances precariously on them, the book resting on the steering wheel.

This is the third time he's driven. His third assignment. It's all gone well so far, he hasn't had any difficulties, but the nausea, the sense of relief when he gets back home, he can sleep for hours. He hasn't told Anna what he's doing, doesn't want to involve her in what he's become a part of. But Ole Rustad *has* become a part of something. A network, silent agreements, codes. He didn't hesitate for a moment that day he had stood up at Ekeberg; he made a decision. He'd given Anna the money he'd received after the operation that day. He felt sick every time he saw his daughters wearing their new dresses, sick to his core. But he smiled.

He's out again today. He's been sent to fetch a "sack," that was how they referred to things: "A sack of turnips." So today someone would be fleeing alone. Last time he'd picked up four people, they'd had a baby with them, a little bundle swaddled in a wool blanket; luckily it had slept the whole way, sedated by sleeping medicine. Even after only two trips he's become familiar with the dangers that can arise. Several of the other drivers have been doing it for a while; he's just a new recruit, but even during his first trips he'd picked up a few tricks to make the process as smooth as possible. He keeps his end of the deal, transports his passengers from A to B, no questions, no conversation, just keeps his car on the road and does his best to make sure that they make it out of the city.

In his mirror Ole Rustad can see someone crossing the road. She looks up and down the empty street and glances all around before fixing her gaze on his vehicle. He returns to his reading, burying his nose in his book while he waits for something to happen.

He hears a click from the back door and she climbs into the car, the sound of hurried breathing from the backseat. He closes his book and sets it down on the passenger seat, turns the key, and hears the hum of the engine as it starts. He turns the wheel to the left, glances in his wing mirror, rolls the car out of the street, moves into second gear, and turns out onto Kirkeveien.

He's heading out of town, to the same place as last time. He knows the way, knows exactly which is the best route to take. The most difficult part is getting out of Oslo without being stopped at a checkpoint. Last time he'd had a close call. The car in front had been waved to the side of the road, there were several more policemen lining the route, but they had signaled to him that he should drive on. It might be different this time, it could be his car made to pull over at the side of the road, it could be him forced to explain who is sitting in the backseat of his vehicle and where they are going. And who is she, exactly? He can't ask, doesn't want to know too much, doesn't want to form a bond with whoever it is in the back of his taxi.

He glides into the outside lane, moves up a gear, and increases his speed. The traffic is moving smoothly today, there aren't too many cars on the road. The whole thing will be over in a matter of hours. He'll make it to bed early tonight.

He can hear the passenger in the backseat moving around, a quiet sound, a slight cough. No, not a cough, a word.

"Ole?" whispers the voice.

He jumps, glances up at the mirror, and swerves into the next lane as if he's never steered a car before. Bloody hell.

He can't turn around, can't look her in the eye. It was hardly any time ago that he had driven the others to the quay, no, he can't think about that, not now, he mustn't say anything. He doesn't know what to say, he's not supposed to speak to the passengers, shouldn't get involved, he's only supposed to change gear and brake and drive, transport them from A to B.

"Gosh, is that really you?" he says, but as soon as it slips out he realizes just how stupid he sounds. He doesn't know what to say, and so he says nothing. Can't force out any more than a grunt, rumbling sounds, doesn't know what they mean or where they come from.

Now he has to concentrate, he has to get a grip. She doesn't say anything either, as if she knows that the situation doesn't lend itself to conversation. There are a thousand things he could ask her, where has she been, does she know anything about her family, Hermann, in fact *he* could tell *her* something about Hermann, about how he had tried to warn him. His hands are clammy around the steering wheel, as if it's the only fixed point of contact in his whole existence.

They're out of the city now. He puts his foot down and drives faster than usual, faster than is strictly legal. The car shakes, the steering wheel vibrates. They're not even halfway and all he wishes is that the journey were over already, he just wants to get home and go to bed. He turns off the main route and takes a minor road, reduces his speed. For the first time he turns around to look at the backseat. Ilse is in the middle, curled up, as if she is making herself as small as she possibly can. They exchange a brief glance before he turns back around and looks out front at the road ahead.

Is there someone there, in the middle of the lane? As he draws closer he sees three figures. Bloody hell. A checkpoint. There are no other cars on the road. He moves into second gear and slows down, as if it might allow him some time to think, might create the opportunity for an explanation to emerge. He can see one of the men signaling to him to stop with long, slow waves toward the side of the road. They're only a few meters away. Down to first gear, the engine whistles, he puts his foot on the brake, the damned trembling in his right hand back once again.

Then something happens. Behind him is a truck. It appears out of nowhere, driving fast. The three policemen stop both vehicles, then split up, with two heading to the truck and one to his taxi. Ole Rustad rolls down his window. The policeman walks toward him, stops a few meters away, turns to his colleagues by the truck, calls out to them, waves his arms, turns back to face the taxi, and continues to make his way over. Ole Rustad sits up straight in his seat, tenses his muscles until his whole body is rigid, stares out the front of his car. There was a name he was supposed to remember. He knows it. They have allies in the police force. He knows there are policemen out there who turn a blind eye where the illegal traffic is concerned. Why can't he remember the name, what the hell was the name? Andersen? Andresen? Antonsen? It was something along those lines. An ordinary, unremarkable surname.

In the mirror he can see the truck driver leaving his cab, walking up alongside his vehicle and undoing the tarpaulin covering the flatbed of the truck. Two of the policemen roll it back. The third continues to approach his car. Ole Rustad waits.

The policeman is beside the taxi, pauses, takes a breath, looks at Ole, looks at Ilse, says nothing. Ole Rustad opens his mouth carefully and lets out a hoarse whisper.

"Isn't it . . . Arnesen?"

The policeman says nothing.

"Arnesen, is that you?"

Ole Rustad tries once more, looking at the policeman.

"Arnesen isn't on duty today," the policeman snaps. "Drive on. And make it quick!"

He raises a hand, gesturing to the two other policemen behind him who have jumped down from the truck flatbed.

Ole Rustad puts his foot on the pedal and the car roars out onto the road once again. In the mirror he sees the truck driver heaving some sacks down from the flatbed for closer inspection by the policemen, who lean over them. Arnesen! He mustn't forget that again. If you are stopped, ask for Arnesen.

They drive through a forest, the trees tall and white alongside the road that bends and snakes, snow falling lightly. Ole Rustad keeps his speed up, turning the steering wheel from side to side, the wipers creaking over the windshield, his foot steady on the accelerator; now he just wants to finish the job. He starts to recognize his surroundings. This was the same way he drove last time too. The road is narrow and icy, the snow piled up in large, heavy drifts. Around the corner he spots the house. Just above the road, it looks so peaceful, a white building that disappears almost entirely into the snowy backdrop.

Ole Rustad reduces his speed and starts to brake. He turns to Ilse, who looks up at him, inquisitive. He knows no more than the fact that his job is done; he has successfully transported his cargo from A to B.

He hears Ilse start to murmur. He looks down as she talks, can't face her, can't process her words. It's not true what she says, there's nothing to thank him for. The nausea returns, it swells deep within him; if only she knew how insincere he really is, sitting there with his hands on the wheel, asking after Arnesen. He can't accept her thanks, but neither can he say anything to stop her. He sits and waits for her to finish, waits for the moment that he can drive back out into the winter's day, shifting gear, steering, braking, stopping. That's all he can do, that's all he ever could do.

A man walks out of the white house, trudging through the deep snow. Ole Rustad opens his mouth, his lips dry, there are words in there, clinging to him, stuck in his throat like a lump he can't cough up. God bless you, God bless, he's never believed a single word about God. He looks at Ilse, his mouth wide open, tongue-tied. Silent.

The man opens the back door.

"Come with me," he says to Ilse.

He watches her walk away. She doesn't turn around. God bless. Ole Rustad spins the car around and back out onto the road, his foot hard on the accelerator.

A WHITE HOUSE, THE MAN, HE'S WEARING a shabby blue set of overalls, his shoelaces untied. His back as he walks away, she just follows him, the snow is deep, where is she, what is happening, everything is so uncertain. The curtains are closed in all of the windows, the paint flaking off, the steps leading up to the front door, she stops on the first one as he grabs the front door handle—she can't go inside, the door creaks.

"Who are you?" Her voice is loud. "Where am I, can you tell me that at least?"

He stares at her.

"Shhh!" he hisses, glancing around, then placing his hand on her back and pushing her inside.

A cramped hallway, work coveralls hanging from pegs, a pair of black rubber boots on the floor, then farther in, a larger room, a staircase, tools laid out on the first few steps; hammers, paint tins, a sledgehammer, garden shears. On the wall hangs a rifle.

"Now listen up, missy."

His voice is low, resolute.

"You can call me Håkon. Like the king. But that's more than enough of your questions for now."

He removes his hat, runs his hands through his hair, loose curls, dark brown, a handsome head of hair that doesn't suit his features.

"You can go in and join the others," he says, nodding toward a door farther on in the room.

The others? He holds the door open, exposing a dimly lit room within. The sound of people breathing. She peers through the doorway and there, just inside, they sit poised, the others, crammed tight in the half-light.

There are many of them, some with blankets wrapped around them, sitting on the floor, on rag rugs, none of them saying a word. A girl lies fast asleep under a blanket, still wearing her hat from which two scruffy braids stick out. A woman rocks a baby agitatedly, glancing around, a gray woolly sock dangling limply from one end of the bundle in her arms. No windows; the air is thick, cold, and yet warm somehow; Ilse sweats and shakes, pulls at the neck of her wool sweater. A single candle is all there is to illuminate the room, it flickers in a candleholder on a table, everything flashing in the light: eyes, blankets, people breathing, people waiting.

"Are you coming to pick potatoes too?"

It is the girl on the floor, she's woken up, she looks up at Ilse, curious.

"Mummy says that's where we're going. I've got a loose tooth, do you want to see?"

She opens her mouth wide and wiggles a tooth in her upper jaw that only just remains attached.

Her mother hushes her, you have to be quiet, she whispers at the floor, the bundle listless in her arms.

Night in the room. Utter darkness. It's not possible to sleep, the floor is hard, she's freezing cold. In the darkness there is so much else that emerges. She stands opposite her mother. Just stands there. That day. She reaches out a hand, feels her mother's cheekbone, hard against her palm, cold, like an egg. The light in the apartment is so soft, so warm, her mother takes her hand, holds it to her face, squeezes her fingers lightly; no one screams anymore, no one shouts, only silence, safe silence, Ilse and her mother.

"But there's snow, how are we supposed to find the potatoes?" The little girl speaks up once again. She's lying just beside Ilse. Ilse can just make out the contours of her face, her mouth. Ilse rolls onto her side, her back to the girl; she doesn't have the answers, not about potatoes or snow or anything at all, for that matter, she only wants to close her eyes, be there, in the apartment with her mother and the soft, warm light.

Håkon walks into the room the following morning. He brings them bottles of milk and slices of bread, handing out a piece to each of them. The lukewarm milk tastes sour, the bread crumbles in her hands, breaking up, the crusts falling away; it tastes of nothing, she's not even hungry.

"My brother has a fever, so he's sleeping."

The girl, she points at the baby, he's lying on the floor now, wrapped up in a blanket, his mother by his side — she tears the bread into tiny pieces and puts them in his mouth.

"Are you all by yourself? Where's your mummy?"

Ilse looks at the girl; she bites off a large chunk of bread, waits for an answer. It's too crowded here, there are too many of them, not enough air, too many difficult questions, she needs to pee, there's a lump in her stomach, she gets up.

Håkon stands in the middle of the room speaking to one of the men. She doesn't know what to ask, she has no voice, no trace of a sound in her entire body. "Sorry," she stammers, looks up at him, at his hair, his eyes, they're pale blue, ". . . the toilet?"

Håkon points at a door at the far side of the room.

"The toilet is outside, behind the house and to the left."

There's a pathway in the snow, deep hollows in the surrounding white. Snowflakes flutter all around, cold on her face, prickly.

Every sound out here is so loud. The snow is wet, she can hear every step; a magpie sits in a tree and calls out before hopping from the branch and disappearing into the white sky. A new sound takes over. A car. Ilse looks to the road: The lights like two sharp eyes, it slows, stops, it's just outside the house. Two men step out, the bang of the car doors as they close, they look at the house, one with a rifle in his hand.

She runs, falls in the snow, runs again, along the path, up the back steps and inside.

"Someone's coming." She shouts, far louder than she should. "They're coming."

Håkon waves his arms, signaling to them all to follow him out of the room, through the hallway; nobody says a word, nobody makes a sound. He grabs his rifle from where it hangs on the wall and points at the stairs, frenzied; there's a door there, in the wall, just under where the staircase curves up toward the next floor. A box room; they crowd inside, Ilse is pressed against the wall with the weight of all the bodies. Håkon closes the door. Jet-black darkness envelops them. He turns a key. He locks them inside.

Breathing, through her nose, short and silent. Voices outside, she can hear them, not the words they're saying, just muffled exchanges. Footsteps in the hallway. Nobody moves. Voices again. Shots. Somebody's firing shots. More shooting. The baby starts to cry. His mother presses her hand over his mouth, forcing the sobs back inside his body.

It falls silent. No car engine, no footsteps in the house, only silence. Someone whispers. He's locked them in. He is the only one with a key. Imagine. Håkon. What if it was Håkon who'd been shot? The baby cries again. His mother drapes the blanket over his head, holds him close to her. We are going to die. A woman speaks out. We'll suffocate in here. She bangs at the door. A man slaps her.

The sound of a key in the lock. They all hold their breath. It's not until they see that it's him that it is released, a deep sigh of accumulated air. Håkon has blood on his overalls, snow up the legs of his trousers, his hair disheveled. They all tumble out of the box room, the light, it's so bright outside. "You have to go, away from here," Håkon says quietly, "now, right away." He points across the room.

"Out the back door. The truck will pick you up. Stay in the forest and wait there for them to come for you."

Outside, just by the path to the toilet, the two bodies piled on top of each other, their eyes open and vacant, the snow red. Ilse looks down, the feet of the person in front of her, her own boots, the tracks in the snow. Everything starts this autumn, she thinks suddenly, one, two, three, four, everything starts this autumn, one, two, three, four, it's silent, afternoon, one, two, three, four, they stop at a ridge, the country road down below. Now all that's left to do is wait.

They stand up as they hear the sound. The truck drives right up alongside the bank of snow, gray and looming, a tarpaulin over the flatbed of the vehicle. A man stands beside the truck, white anorak, woolly hat, "you can call me Håkon," he says, "like the king." He unties the ropes that keep the tarpaulin in place. "There are full burlap sacks in the back, hide as best you can." The scent of wood from the sacks, Ilse crouches down on her haunches, feels the way the vehicle rattles as they drive, the draft blasting through the gaps in the tarpaulin. The scent from the sacks, from her woolly sweater, Maridalen, suddenly she's there, inside the cabin, Hermann, he's there too, where is he now? The vehicle stops.

"Are we at the potatoes now?" She whispers from behind a sack, the little girl; her mother doesn't answer. The second man to go by the name of Håkon leads them through a forest, white trees, snowflakes sprinkling from them, resting on their eyelashes, melting, her tights wet. They stop by a body of water, a lake.

Håkon murmurs in hushed tones. "You have to spread out," he says, looking from one face to the next.

"If any of you are discovered, the others can still make it across."

The ice. Solid beneath their feet.

Everything around them is white. The light in the sky. The sound of the others. The snow. Fragments, like tiny scraps of paper.

The country just ahead of them. The thought of it. Sweden. Everything that awaits them there. Everything that has disappeared.

Everything that no longer exists.

Everything. Only white.

WINTER IS OVER.

Everything. Spring. It'll soon be summer.

The leaves line the branches, forcing their way into the light. Green, lush. Resplendent, insistent. Like heart tissue. The air is soft and tinged with something, a scent, a rupture. The insects buzz, quiver.

The warmth of the sun falls on her face, scorching; it is as if she hasn't been properly warm in a long time, her body under a thin layer of ice, still, in waiting. She has been in Sweden for two and a half years. Thirty months. Nine hundred and twelve days, she has counted each and every one. Thinking of this moment as she has gone to school and worked and eaten and dreamed and laughed and cried. Thinking about precisely this; coming here again, coming home.

Toftes gate lies before her like an avenue; all it takes is for her to walk over, up and along. On the corner of Biermanns gate she stops. She stands there motionless for a few minutes. All the time she's waited, the images

269

in her mind. The dreams a little while ago. Everything she never dreamed, the dreams she forgot, those yet to come. Those that ask. Those that answer. Those that make it round the corner on Toftes gate and go no farther. No farther than this.

The light falls at a diagonal through the gate. The backyard is bathed in bright sunlight. An empty shell, four floors, a wall of bricks and open windows. The gate is open. The passageway just inside.

The rubbish bins are still pushed up against the wall, no stench from within them anymore. She can see the lilac tree at the back of the yard, the bench beneath the branches; it has changed color. There's someone there, in the backyard, she can hear laughter, a rippling sound, a little boy running around with a ball, a man on a chair. He sits with his back to her, but even so, she recognizes him. He turns as she walks into the yard, remains in his seat and looks at her for a moment before his face breaks into a smile.

"Oh my goodness, it's you!" Ole Rustad says, standing up. "You're a young lady now!"

He walks her way, opens his arms, an embrace without embracing as he looks at her without looking. The little boy starts to cry. His ball has become trapped beneath the bicycle rack.

"What's his name?" she asks, nodding in the direction of the little boy.

"This is little Ole. He turned two at Christmas."

The boy walks toward them. He stands behind his father, clutching at his trouser leg.

"We've another on the way." Ole pats the boy on the head. "Tell her your name, Ole," he teases.

"Ole," the little boy says, thrusting his finger up his snotty nose.

Ole Rustad stands there beaming.

"Well well well," he says, glancing out over the backyard. "Well well well."

Her window up there, open, a white curtain fluttering through the gap, flapping in the light breeze.

"There are others living there now," Ole says. "They moved in a while after you . . ."

He stands for a moment, simply nodding.

The apartment, she can picture every room so clearly. The narrow hallway, coats and jackets and hats, the kitchen, her mother over the stove, the smell of roasting meat, baking, the scent of her mother. The living room with the round table, the candles lit, her father in the armchair by the window, whistling, humming, the mirror hanging between the two windows.

"It's been good," Ole says, lighting a cigarette. "Lately, I mean. We went down to see the king when he came. You should have seen it, Ilse. What a celebration."

He blows the smoke out through his nostrils, looks at her, uncertain.

The windows to the right. Hermann's windows, they're closed.

"You should go up and knock, you know," Ole says, throwing away his cigarette, stepping on it, picking up his son and walking to the door. "It was good to see you," he smiles, opening the door and going inside.

The backyard, so quiet. Yet so full of sound. Birds. A bee. The clanking of cooking pots from one kitchen or another. The tram from Vogts gate on its way downtown. Breathing. And then. A window opening. The third floor.

"Ilse Stern!"

His head up there. His thick, fair hair. A hand that waves, that lovely hand. A smile.

Hermann Rød. She says. Inside.

"Wait for me, Ilse," he calls, closing the window.

The sun on the rooftop. A big yellow circle. Long beams reaching outward. The grass smells fresh and dry. Before long the backyard will be filled with yellow, rotting leaves, before long the wind will blow again, and the rain will pour down, hammering against the asphalt, creating deep furrows in the gravel. Before long everything will become white and cold, a hard shell forming over everything that is dead.

But now.

The thud of the door. He's coming. Out of the door. Out into the sunlight. Out of the apartment block. From the outside it looks like any other building.

AFTERWORD

On April 9, 1940, Norway was occupied by Germany and remained under German control until May 8, 1945. Even though there were no battlefields in Norway during the Second World War, such as there were in France or Belgium, these five years under occupation left their mark on the Norwegian population. There was a shortage of food, and goods were rationed. People were subjected to strict controls and censorship. Many joined the resistance movement, working against the Germans by taking part in illegal intelligence work, sabotage, and various other types of action. Some joined the Germans by allying themselves with the Norwegian fascist party, Nasjonal Samling (NS). For the large majority, daily life was characterized by uncertainty, fear for the future, food shortages, and a fight to make ends meet, yet there was also a strong solidarity and sense of belonging among those affected.

The Norwegian Jews were subjected to a steadily increasing stream of harassment from the NS and the Germans from the very start of the occupation. In 1942 this further intensified, with all Jews having their identification papers stamped with a red letter J and being required to fill in a form with information about themselves. The information gathered as part of this campaign offered German and Norwegian authorities a greater overview of the Jews in Norway, which proved crucial to the mass arrests that took place in the autumn of 1942.

The persecution of the Jews in Norway was systematic, carried out on specific dates and at specific times. On the morning of October 26, 1942, male Jews over the age of fifteen were arrested. Exactly one month later, on the morning of November 26, 1942, women and children were taken. The German ship *Donau* sailed from Oslo on the afternoon of that same day with 532 Norwegian Jews on board. Only nine of those were to survive Auschwitz.

The characters in *Almost Autumn* are fictional, but the story is based on real events that took place in Oslo in the autumn of 1942. My starting point for this book was to investigate the notion of chance. It struck me that the persecution of the Jews was so systematic and time-specific in its enforcement that chance must also have played some part in events. What if someone wasn't at home on that particular morning of November 26? What if, by some twist of fate, one member of the family wasn't there to be taken? And how significant would the consequences be? I read several stories about people who escaped arrest, purely through chance, managing to make it to safety in neutral Sweden. I wanted *Almost Autumn* to build on this notion of chance.

I have grown up with stories of the Second World War. My grandfather Einar spent three years in a concentration camp in Japan, while my grandfather Edvard was active in the intelligence organization XU. Uncle Ole secretly kept a pig in his cellar that they slaughtered for a traditional Christmas dinner. Uncle Kolbjørn helped fugitives make it over to Sweden. My grandmother Randi had to leave her home when the Germans occupied the property, while my grandmother Astrid was a midwife who became unpopular after helping some German women in labor.

They told me about their lives during the war, and I found their stories exhilarating. It felt as if the distance created by time had been erased, as if I had been through these experiences myself. I recall my grandfather's identification tag, kept in a drawer of my grandmother's bureau, and I remember sitting there, holding it in my hand, feeling the fabric, smelling it, looking at his identification number, and imagining all that he must have experienced while he was imprisoned in Japan. It was only by chance that he survived. Perhaps the idea of exploring chance the way that I have in *Almost*

Autumn is connected to my own history. If my grandfather hadn't survived those three years in Japan, then I wouldn't be here.

All the older members of my family are dead now. Soon there will be nobody left to talk about their own experiences of the Second World War. I feel as if it is important that our stories of the war are passed on to the next generation. *Almost Autumn* is my small attempt to do just that.

Marianne Kaurin
Nesodden, Norway
March 8, 2016

For more information on World War II and the
Holocaust in Norway:

Center for Studies of Holocaust and Religious
Minorities
http://www.hlsenteret.no/english/

Oslo Jewish Museum
http://oslojewishmuseum.no/

MARIANNE KAURIN was born in 1974 in Tønsberg, Norway. She studied at the Norwegian Institute of Children's Books, and her debut novel, *Almost Autumn*, received the Norwegian Ministry of Culture prize, and was named Young People's Book of the Year in a vote by students from all over Norway. Marianne now lives just outside of Oslo in Nesodden with her husband and three children, and is an editor of educational literature for high school students.

ROSIE HEDGER was born in Scotland and completed her MA (with Honors) in Scandinavian studies at the University of Edinburgh. As part of her undergraduate studies, Rosie spent a year at the University of Oslo, and later lived and worked in Sweden and Denmark before returning to the UK, where she is now based. Find Rosie online at www.rosiehedger.com.

This book was edited by Emily Clement and designed by Elizabeth B. Parisi. The text was set in Sabon LT Roman, a typeface designed by Adobe. The book was printed and bound at RR Donnelley in Crawfordsville, Indiana. Production was supervised by Rebekah Wallin and manufacturing was supervised by Angelique Browne.